*A
Harlequin
Romance*

OTHER
Harlequin Romances
by JANICE GRAY

1167—DEAR BARBARIAN
1230—CROWN OF CONTENT
1275—SHAKE OUT THE STARS
1707—GARDEN OF THE SUN
1744—WINTER LOVING
1852—STAR LIGHT, STAR BRIGHT

TAKE ALL MY LOVES

by

JANICE GRAY

HARLEQUIN BOOKS   TORONTO
WINNIPEG

Original hard cover edition published in 1969
by Mills & Boon Limited.

© Janice Gray 1969

SBN 373-01886-X

Harlequin edition published June 1975

Printed in Canada

1886

CHAPTER ONE

THERE was complete silence in the little studio. The artist, a grey-haired man with bowed shoulders, stood at his easel, completely absorbed in his work. From time to time he glanced at the slender, boyish figure curled up in a nearby armchair, but he did not speak.

Peta, her hands cupping her chin, watched him with growing impatience. She was nearly nineteen, but she looked much younger, and she was dressed in her customary slacks and chunky sweater, with her chestnut hair tumbling untidily on to her shoulders. Her face was not a pretty one by conventional standards, but the sparkling hazel eyes, short nose, delicately arched brows and wide, sweet-lipped mouth added up to an ensemble which reflected a lively intelligence and an eager, frank, adventurous spirit. It was an extraordinarily transparent, expressive face and just at the moment boredom was beginning to register very plainly indeed.

Cautiously she wriggled one foot. It was agony for her to have to sit still for any length of time, but every movement brought such a heavy frown to the artist's face that she felt she would rather endure the torment of pins and needles than run the risk of incurring his wrath.

This time, however, although he saw her move he merely laughed and flung down his brush.

"All right, my dear! The light's too bad for me to do any more. You've behaved very well." He rubbed his hand across his sunken eyes, realising with astonishment that it was far later than he had thought. He knew Peta's restless temperament and had not expected a long sitting, any more than he would have expected to imprison a wild bird. "Tired?"

"Only of sitting still!" Peta stretched herself with a sigh of heartfelt relief. She jumped up and began to wander round the wildly untidy studio, picking her way carefully round the jumble of bottles and tubes, canvases, palettes and rags, but typically she made no attempt to see how the artist had pictured her. "I'm jolly glad I'm not a professional model! May I go now, please?"

"Yes, but I'm afraid I haven't nearly finished. Is it too much to ask you to spare me another hour or so? At the weekend, perhaps?" He spoke diffidently, knowing full well that although London was full of beautiful women who would have been only too flattered and delighted to have had their portraits painted by him, this strange child was not at all impressed by the honour he had shown her. Nevertheless, he had not bargained for her swift, unhesitating refusal.

"I'm sorry, I can't. Not this weekend." Then, sensing his disappointment, she added a quick explanation. "My guardian is coming home from abroad, you see. Ann—I ought to call her Aunt Ann, really, but I never do—won't like it if I'm not around to welcome him." She grimaced as she spoke. It was only too evident that the prospect was not at all to her liking.

Richard Mayne's lined, parchment-like face showed his surprise.

"You have no parents, my dear?"

Peta shook her head. She perched herself on the edge of a table, swinging her long legs and looking up at him with laughing eyes. "It's obvious you don't indulge in gossip, Mr. Mayne. If you did your daily help would have kept you well informed. She likes to pride herself that she knows everything that there is to be known about everyone in the village!"

"I can well believe it!" Richard Mayne spoke with feeling. Mrs. Davies was a good cook and looked after him well, but she talked far too much. Not that he ever listened. He simply wasn't interested. The whole idea of this Norfolk sabbatical was to get away from people altogether. He had had enough of them—and of the kind of life that the London specialist had told him was killing him. Here in this small village that he had known and loved as a small boy he had meant to go into complete retreat, but Peta had changed his mind for him. He had been doing some sketching by the river when he had caught sight of her at the helm of a small

6

dinghy, cheeks glowing, eyes sparkling, hair blown wildly back, facing the wind with gallantry and joy, and he had known at once that whatever happened there was a face he wanted to paint.

Now, sinking down into a chair, he said drily, "Since it hadn't occurred to me to ask Mrs. Davies for your life history I take it that you're going to take pity on my ignorance? Tell me about your guardian."

Peta laughed. "It's nice of you to be interested. There isn't much to tell, though. He doesn't come home very often, so everything gets left to poor Ann. He's an archaeologist—an *eminent* archaeologist." There was a hint of mischief in her face as she hastily corrected herself. "He's been in Peru for the last three years. Before that he was in Greece, and before that in Egypt. Wherever there's been an ancient civilisation, there you'll find Professor Devlin!"

"I see." Richard Mayne looked at her. "I must say that it certainly doesn't sound as though he's taken his duties as guardian very seriously."

"Oh!" Peta flushed and looked away. "That's hardly fair. I oughtn't to have been dumped on him at all, really. My parents named him as my guardian because they had to do things in a hurry and they simply couldn't think of anybody else, but of course they didn't really expect anything to happen to them. Then the plane taking them to Paris caught fire in mid-air. . . ." She paused for a moment, and then went on, "It must have been an awful shock for the poor man, to find that he was suddenly responsible for a ten-year-old girl. He was quite middle-aged, you know, and a confirmed bachelor. There was nothing else he could do but send me here to his sister. Luckily she didn't mind."

She might have added, but didn't, that there was very little that Ann *did* mind. She was a placid soul whose all-absorbing interest was her garden: providing Peta kept out of mischief she had always left her to do pretty much as she pleased.

Richard Mayne's expression was slightly sardonic. "Well, what brings your Professor to Norfolk now? Has he run out of pyramids or has someone uncovered

7

an Ancient Monument in the middle of the marshland?"

Peta laughed. "No such luck! We've got St. Benet's
Abbey and that's our lot, I think."

"Then why—?"

"Oh, apparently he's made some quite important discoveries in Peru and he thinks he ought to write a book
about them. He needs peace and quiet for that, so I
suppose Greylings is ideal."

Peta's voice betrayed her utter lack of interest and
the man gave her an amused look.

"You don't sound very enthusiastic."

"I'm not," she owned. "We've never got on very well
together, I'm afraid. He'd have liked me to be a blue-
stocking, and of course I'm nothing of the sort." She
sighed. "I've got an awful feeling that there are going
to be ructions when he finds out about my job!"

"What do you do? Sell icecream to visitors?"
Richard Mayne asked, laughing.

"Nearly as bad. I teach people to sail. It's a School
at Wroxham, it was only started this season and it's
terrific fun." Peta's face and voice were eager. "I love
the job and Major and Mrs. Nowell—they're my
employers—are dears, but I don't suppose my scholarly,
distinguished guardian will approve. He'd never agree
with the Water Rat that 'There's nothing—absolutely
nothing—half so much worth doing as simply messing
about in boats'! And of course he's bound to ask what's
going to happen during the winter—everyone does."

"What about Ann? Didn't she oppose your plans?"

Peta shook her head. "Ann was a darling. She always
understands. She knew quite well I couldn't stand the
thought of being cooped up in four walls all day long. I
can't bear to be caged . . . fenced in. I need the sun on
my face and the wind against me!"

"Wide open spaces, in fact!" the man laughed. "But
what about money?"

"Oh, I get wages, of course! Not very much because
the Norwells can't afford it: it's a new venture, you
see, and we've got to build it up. But I don't mind. I
don't need a lot: I haven't got extravagant tastes!"

She glanced at her watch. "Heavens, is that really the time? I simply must go now, Mr. Mayne. I meant to go sailing with Mike this evening: I'd like to try and catch him before he goes home."

Her vitality was like a pure flame, Richard Mayne thought, half enviously. Aloud he said, "It was good of you to give up your plans for me. Is Mike the young Viking I saw you with yesterday?"

Peta looked at him with approval. "That's a jolly good description of him! Yes, that was Mike. He's my best friend: we've known each other for years." She gave him a radiant smile. "Goodbye. I'll come and sit for you again, I promise! But not until next week!"

Outside the studio she drew a deep breath, rejoicing that she was once more out in the open air. It would soon be dusk. The sun was already beginning to sink and both sky and land seemed to be aflame with red and golden fire. She'd *wasted* a whole evening, when she might have been out on the river with Mike! She wished now that she'd never gone anywhere near the studio! Only Mr. Mayne was rather a dear, and she'd found it impossible to say "No" when he'd asked her to sit for him, reluctant though she had been. Conscious of her own youth and glowing health, she was pitiful of his frailty and disturbed by the way in which his rather hard grey eyes so often reflected a weary disillusionment. She wondered why he felt like that. Perhaps people didn't want to buy his pictures, though that was hardly likely. Some of the Norfolk landscapes he had shown her were gorgeous, and there was one, of wild geese silhouetted against a sky like this, illuminated by a tide of gold, which she'd love to hang in her bedroom.

For a moment her face was very sober as she thought of the tired, elderly man she had left behind her in the studio, then, with a characteristic shrug of her slim shoulders, she took to her heels and began racing towards the river. With any luck Mike would only just have got back from wherever he'd been.

The Dyke was crowded, though since it was the height of the season that was hardly surprising. Peta walked quickly up the river wall, her eyes searching for

Mike's dinghy among the boats of all types and sizes which were moored alongside the bank. Furled sails surgarloaf white against a background of crimsoning sky and shadowed marshland . . . muddy river water touched with flame . . . the fragrance of coffee and fried bacon as holidaymakers in cabin cruisers prepared their suppers . . . masts dipping and swaying to the movements of the water which lapped gently against the gleaming enamelled hulls . . . but no *Romany*. Hadn't Mike returned yet? Or had he moored the dinghy somewhere else?

Then she saw him. Hands thrust deep into the pockets of his ancient flannels, the sun gilding his fair hair, he came striding to meet her and she thought again how apposite Richard Mayne's description had been.

"Hi! Where've you been? I thought you were coming out with me this evening. I've had a marvellous trip: wind just right!"

"I'm sorry, Mike. I've been with Mr. Mayne." Peta felt another sharp pang of regret for her wasted opportunity. Sailing with Mike was her greatest joy. As she had told Richard Mayne, they were close friends: the three years' difference in their ages hardly mattered and she had always been accustomed to look upon him as an elder brother.

Mike's brows lifted. "That queer old artist chap you've chummed up with? What on earth for?"

"He—he wanted to paint me." Peta flushed and spoke a little shyly, for she thought that it must sound so absurd. Why, it wasn't even as though she was pretty!

Evidently Mike agreed, for he looked frankly incredulous. "Paint *you*? For heaven's sake why?"

Peta shook her head. "I don't know. He just took it into his head that he wanted to and I didn't like to say no. I—I feel rather sorry for him, Mike. He's old, and I don't believe he's a bit well."

Mike looked amused, but also faintly irritated, as he always was whenever Peta had an interest he did not share.

"Well, you needn't flatter yourself that he picked you

10

for your looks! I expect he knows a mug when he sees one—anyone else would make him pay fifteen bob an hour!" he said with brotherly candour.

Peta laughed. Completely without vanity, she saw no reason to resent his frankness.

"Goodness, I'm not in the least flattered! I'd have much rather been on the river with you! How far did you go?"

"Oh, not too far. I promised Mum faithfully that I wouldn't be late for supper." He looked at his watch. "Which reminds me. We'd better get a move on: she's expecting you as well. Your favourite—mixed grill, so don't say no!"

"I wasn't going to," Peta said cheerfully. "Smelling all this bacon frying has made me feel ravenous!"

Unselfconsciously she linked her arm in his. With one last lingering glance behind them, they turned and began to walk briskly along the river wall that bordered the long Dyke. A keen wind, blowing across the flat marshes, stung their cheeks, but they hardly noticed it. To them it was part of their East Coast heritage: they had grown up with it just as they had grown up with each other.

Mike was the first to break their companionable silence. "How's the sailing school getting on?"

"Fine, thanks. We had two new pupils today, one a rather nice girl and the other a ghastly know-it-all. You should have seen the mess she tried to get us into!"

Mike laughed. "I'm glad I didn't! You've more patience than I have, Peta. I wouldn't teach anyone to sail for love or money!"

"I like it, though of course it's much nicer being on one's own or with somebody experienced. Are you taking *Romany* out tomorrow?"

Mike shook his head. "Can't be managed, I'm afraid. I'm hoping to do a spot of racing at Horning on Saturday, though. You'll crew for me, won't you?" It was more of a statement than a question. What had happened tonight was exceptional: Peta never missed a chance to sail with him if she could possibly help it.

"Oh!" She looked at him in dismay, some of the

glow dying out of her small, vivid face. "I—I'd love to, Mike, but I may not be able to. You know who's comming home on Saturday. I told you ages ago!"

Mike frowned. "Oh, of course! I'd forgotten for a moment." He paused, then added lightly "You've been a free agent for so long that it's difficult to think of you with a stern guardian in the background!"

Peta smiled briefly but did not answer. In spite of herself she could not help feeling apprehensive about the Professor's homecoming, for she was not quite sure how the pattern of her days would be affected. She felt that he was bound to be critical of the vigorous open-air life she led, and that at the first opportunity he would start talking about college and a "suitable" career. How could she possibly make him understand that she did not want either?

Mike's voice broke into her thoughts as they reached the bottom of the Dyke.

"You know, I can't remember much about the old chap, except that he usually looked rather grumpy and you always seemed to be in his bad books for some reason or other!"

"I know. It used to worry poor Ann dreadfully. I could never do anything right."

Peta's voice was rueful and Mike laughed. "You were too much of a tomboy, I guess. Maybe things will be different this time."

"I doubt it. I wish to goodness he'd stayed in Peru," Peta said gloomily, and Mike laughed again and gave her arm a reassuring squeeze.

"If things get too bad you can always seek sanctuary with us. After all, we've more or less adopted you already!" he said comfortingly.

That was true—or almost. She had always been made welcome at Mike's home and she was on the best of terms with his younger brother and sister, Dickon and Holly. The only snag was that she never felt completely at ease with his beautiful, elegant widowed mother. Mrs. Mandeville had always been pleasant, but she was a countrywoman by necessity rather than by inclination, disliked sailing and found most rural activities boring, so that unfortunately she and Peta had little in common.

Mike had parked his ancient sports car in a yard belonging to a friendly farmer, for although Peta's home was a mere stone's throw from the river his own was two or three miles distant. He opened the door for Peta to climb in and had just tucked his own long, loose-limbed frame behind the driving wheel when a cheery voice hailed him.

"It's Bob." Mike's face creased into his ready smile and he stuck his head out of the window as he saw the burly figure of the farmer making his way towards the car. He and Bob Dyall had a friendship which stretched back over many years and at one time he had even thought of making farming his own career.

The idea had come to nothing, but his interest remained. Watching his intent face as he talked to Bob, Peta thought with a pang, "How can he bear it . . . being cooped up in a stuffy office when once he wanted something so different?" She knew that Mike's one ambition when he left school had been to go to an agricultural college and take a course in farm management, but he had reckoned without his mother's bitter opposition. A waste of a first-class education, she had called it, and Mike, knowing the sacrifices she had made in order to send him to Winchester, his father's old school, and unwilling to cause her unhappiness, had reluctantly given way to her pleadings. Now he was articled to a firm of solicitors in Norwich and travelled backwards and forwards daily: he seemed to be quite happy and of course he hadn't lost everything, he still had the sailing he loved, but Peta felt that just occasionally he regretted his lost opportunities.

Bob and Mike had finished their conversation. Bob, with a cheery wave of his hand in Peta's direction, stumped off in the direction of his cowsheds, and the car roared into life as Mike stabbed the starter button.

"Good old Bob. Wish there were a few more around like him." Mike said as they swept through the tiny village with its cluster of thatched cottages, one or two large farmhouses and picturesque Norman church. "He really is the salt of the earth, or whatever that saying is."

Peta laughed. "He's certainly been a good friend to us. We must have been an awful nuisance to him at times, some of the things we did when we were small, but he never let on to your mother or Aunt Ann!"

"No, but he gave me a jolly good hiding once or twice!" Mike said, grinning. "Remember the time we lit a camp-fire too close to one of his haystacks?"

Peta gave a reminiscent shiver. That particular escapade had taken place in the field they were just passing. Mike was driving along the narrow, winding lanes at a steady pace but was resisting the temptation to speed: better be late for supper than land up in a ditch, and that was what was quite likely to happen if anyone travelling too fast were to meet another vehicle. Visitors were the main hazard: the 'locals' all knew that whenever two vehicles met the chances were that someone would be forced to back up until the road widened sufficiently for the other to pass.

Peta, looking out of the open window at the shadowy patchwork of fields and hedges, wondered if there would ever come a time when she would fail to be enchanted by the shapes and colours, the scents and sounds of the countryside which had woven such a happy background to her life for so long.

She drew a deep breath and said inconsequentially, "Fancy anyone bothering to poke about in mouldy old ruins when they could be *growing* things!"

"Hear, hear." Mike swung off the lane into a curved drive as he spoke and brought the car to a stop in front of his home.

Cedar Lodge was a small, modernised cottage with grey stone walls, small lattice windows and a neat thatched roof, and everyone with the exception of Mrs. Mandeville thought it was charming. As far as she was concerned its disadvantages by far outweighed its virtues: it was in an out-of-the-way position, the ceilings were too low, the rooms were poky and there really wasn't enough space for a family of four. Many people, hearing her grumble, felt tempted to ask why in that

14

case she stayed, but of course the answer was that she could afford nothing better. Her husband had died when Mike was only thirteen, leaving her with only a small income and precious little capital. Since it was obvious that she could no longer afford to keep up the luxurious London flat for which they paid an exorbitant rent it had seemed providential when an elderly relative had written offering them a country cottage, rent-free, for as long as they wanted it. The prospect of living in rural surroundings had appalled her, but her straitened circumstances had made refusal impossible. There could be no question of her taking a job—she had had no training of any kind—and living in the country would, she knew, be far cheaper than living in Town. As far as the children were concerned she had had no qualms: she was sure they would soon adapt themselves to their new life. Events had proved her right, and it was only she who had found it impossible to fit into the tight-knit little village community and only she who still sighed for the pleasures of urban life.

She thought Peta, with her tomboy ways and love of boats and wide-open spaces, an odd child, but she was quite fond of her and greeted her warmly when Mike brought her into the tiny kitchen where she was putting the finishing touches to the evening meal.

"My goodness! Wonders will never cease! I must say that though I wanted you home in time for supper I never expected you before midnight! What happened? Were you sea-sick or did *Romany* spring a leak?"

"Listen to the woman!" Mike said indignantly. "I'll have you know, Mother, that as of this moment *Romany* is about the best boat on the Broads!"

"She goes like a bird!" Peta, as fond of *Romany* as was Mike himself, backed him up loyally. "You should come with us some time, Mrs. Mandeville. You don't know what you're missing!"

"Oh yes, I do! As far as I'm concerned sailing is strictly for fools and brave men!" Margaret Mandeville spoke with feeling. Small and dark, with patrician features and an indefinable air of elegance, she barely came up to her elder son's shoulder. It was not from

15

her that Mike had inherited either his height or his fair good looks: he very definitely took after his father's side of the family.

"Which category do we belong to?" Mike mocked. He investigated the contents of a saucepan on the stove, sniffing with pleasure the appetising smell. Margaret cooked superbly—in fact, everything she did she did supremely well. "I'm beginning to be extremely glad we *aren't* late! Where are the kids?"

"Here." Dickon and Holly bounced into the room, right on cue. In their case they did resemble their mother, both in features and colouring, and as there was only a year's difference between them they were frequently taken for twins. Neither shared their elder brother's enthusiasm for sailing: Dickon preferred horses and Holly, who was feminine to the core, adored ballet.

"Peta! Will you come and help me with my jigsaw?" Holly seized hold of Peta's hand. "I want to finish it before bedtime and you're awfully good at finding the difficult pieces!"

"No, wait till after supper. It's nearly ready isn't it, Mum?" Dickon, who claimed that he was always on the point of starving, felt that his sister had got her priorities wrong.

"It is. And your turn to lay the table," his mother said firmly.

Dickon sighed. It was a job he hated, but he knew that if he made a fuss he might get landed with something worse, like the drying up. He went out, but reappeared almost immediately. He had just remembered something he wanted to tell Peta.

"Say, Peta, did you know there was something about your old Professor in yesterday's paper?"

Peta's eyes widened. "No, I didn't. There wasn't anything in ours. What did it say?" Instinctively she looked towards Mike.

"Haven't a clue. Nobody showed it to me," Mike said comfortably.

"Oh, there were only a couple of paragraphs about the discoveries he's made in Peru." It was Margaret

Mandeville who answered. "He's in New York at the moment, isn't he? There was rather a good picture of him at the airport, just stepping off the plane. Go and see if you can find the paper, Dickon, it's probably with today's."

Dickon darted off, but came back looking regretful.

"It isn't there. Somebody must have used it for something."

"Oh well, it doesn't matter!" Peta said cheerfully. "I know what the old dear looks like and I don't suppose he's changed very much in the last few years!"

"Except to get a bit greyer and dustier!" Holly said with her impudent grin. "Isn't it funny how nearly all archaeologists manage to look sort of shrivelled up and mummified?

"I've only ever once seen a photograph of one who looked different: he was a real sex-pot! I wouldn't have in the least minded going on a dig with *him*!"

"Precocious brat!" Mike said disapprovingly, and indeed Holly, at thirteen, was more knowledgeable in some ways than Peta, nearly six years her senior.

Holly tilted her curly dark head and looked at him saucily, but before she could answer her mother interposed.

"I'm sorry about the paper, I meant to save it, but right now there are more important things to think about. Do you want to wash your hands before supper, Peta? And Mike, please go and take off those disgusting flannels and change into something decent! Dickon, we can't have supper until the table is laid, so if you're hungry you'd better hurry up!"

She heaved a sigh of relief as the kitchen rapidly emptied. When the whole family was congregated in its tiny area there simply wasn't room to breathe! She turned back to the stove thinking: If only the cottage belonged to us we could sell it and move a bit nearer Norwich. . . . Mike really ought to be living there now, he doesn't meet anyone worthwhile in this benighted village and all he seems to think about is sailing that wretched boat! He ought to be going to parties and leading a proper social life . . . after all, in his profession

17

the right contacts can be so important! Her thoughts ran on in this habitual manner until her daughter's pensive voice suddenly provided her with an alarming check.

"I wonder when Mike and Peta will decide to get married?"

Her mother turned in a flash, astonishment and something akin to fear in her dark eyes.

"Married? Mike and Peta? What *are* you talking about, you silly child?"

"I'm not a silly child!" Holly sounded indignant. "Everyone says they'll get married some day! I even heard Mrs. Evans tell someone that they were ideally suited, and *she's* the Vicar's wife! So there!"

Margaret Mandeville felt just as though she had been delivered a body-blow, but with a tremendous effort she recovered her composure.

"Don't be rude, Holly!" she said crisply. "And whatever the village tabby-cats may say, please don't repeat their stupid remarks here—and especially not in front of Mike or Peta! They've got about as much intention of marrying as the cow has of jumping over the moon, but there's no need to make either of them feel embarrassed or self-conscious. It would be a pity to spoil a very good friendship!"

Holly looked at her, bewildered by the unaccustomed sharpness of her voice. She wanted to say that there was nothing she would like better than to have Peta for a sister, but she had the sense to keep quiet. She had rarely seen her mother looking so upset.

Margaret, a little red spot burning in each of her cheeks, took a pile of warm plates out of the oven and was aware that her hands were trembling. Mike—and Peta? No and no and *no*, she thought passionately. Wild little Peta, with her gaucherie and complete lack of sophistication was not the wife she wanted for her eldest son! Marriage between them would be an utter disaster—oh, not for them, perhaps, but it would certainly sound the death-knoll of her own cherished hopes. More than for either of her two younger children she was ambitious for Mike, who with his looks, his charm and his brains, had such excellent potential. But not if he married someone like Peta! She'd let him spend the rest of his life in this dull little backwater!

The worst of it was, she thought, ladling crisp golden chips into a Wedgwood tureen, that she'd never even dreamed of such a possibility. Perhaps she'd been too blind, too complacent—but Peta had been part of their lives for so long, she and Mike had been like brother and sister for years! And even now, though she must be nearly nineteen, Peta was still an utter child, completely unawakened. It was practically certain that she had never once looked upon Mike as a possible husband, only as a friend and comrade. But . . . ! If people were beginning to wonder and conjecture, if the idea was once put into her head. . . . !

She felt sunk in depression. She'd already fought Mike once, and although she had won she did not want to have to fight him again. Far better to remove the danger before it threatened—though that was easier said than done. It wasn't as if Mike was interested in any other girls, he said they bored him. And as for Peta . . . why, even Holly knew more about the attractions of the opposite sex than did Peta!

She heard Mike's voice and then Peta's with its eager warmth, answering him, and her lips compressed as she began to untie the strings of her dainty flowered overall. There might well be nothing at all to worry about, but for her own peace of mind she intended to make quite, quite sure. And though she certainly didn't want anyone to be hurt, it was just possible, just remotely possible, that Peta's elderly guardian, now on his way to his Norfolk birthplace, might prove to be the very ally she so badly needed.

CHAPTER TWO

PETA came down to breakfast the following morning to find Ann, who was a tall, angular woman with faded blue eyes and rough grey hair, standing by the window reading a letter. She and Peta rarely used the big, gloomy dining room with its dark-panelled walls and heavy furniture and ate most of their meals in the kitchen, which was sunnier and far more cheerful-looking. It had colour-washed walls and heavy oak beams crossing the ceiling, a huge dresser with blue willow-pattern china, rush matting on the red tiled floor and high-backed, rush-seated chairs.

"Morning, Ann! Sorry I'm late!" Peta greeted the elder woman cheerfully as she sat down at the big oak table and immediately helped herself to toast and coffee. She didn't often oversleep, but she had had a very late night. Something had gone wrong with Mike's car on the way home, and after wasting the best part of an hour desperately trying to re-start it, they'd been forced to push it into the nearest gateway and walk the rest of the way to Greylings. Goodness only knew what time poor Mike had eventually got home! He would probably have to borrow his mother's car to get to work today.

"Good morning, dear." Ann answered her mechanically, but something in her voice made Peta give her a sharp look.

"What's the matter? Anything wrong, Ann?"

Ann's plain, kind, square-jawed face, with its sunburnt weatherbeaten skin, was unusually flushed.

"No—yes—oh, I don't know! It's John. This letter is from him, to say—oh, it really is too bad of him! So inconsiderate! And at such short notice, too!"

Peta stared at her in amazement. Normally her aunt was placidity itself and nothing ever disturbed her: whatever had her brother written to provoke such indignant incoherence?

"What's the matter?" she repeated patiently.

20

Ann pushed her short grey hair nervously back from her flushed face.

"John's not coming alone. He's bringing two people with him. A secretary, and the man who's been with him in Peru!"

"*Here*?" Ann's dismay was now reflected in Peta's expressive face. "Oh, Ann, no! How ghastly! Why didn't he tell you before? And how long are they going to stay?"

"Read it." Ann handed her the letter.

Mercifully it was short: Professor Devlin's writing was not noted for its legibility. The words danced in front of Peta's eyes.

I thought I had better let you know that I have invited my friend and colleague, Dr. Nicholas Waring, who has been of invaluable assistance to me on my recent expedition, to spend a week or two with us at Greylings. He is at present recovering from a very severe attack of malaria which confined him to bed for several days, and I feel that a strong dose of Norfolk air will probably do him a great deal of good. Unfortunately, however, I must leave the question of his entertainment to you and to Peta, for I shall, of course, be fully occupied with my book. I intend to start upon this as soon as possible and in order to expedite matters I have decided to engage a secretary to whom I shall dictate as and when I can and who will be responsible for sorting through my notes and preparing the typescript for publication and so on. Naturally Miss Kent will expect to live as one of the family, but I am certain that this will present no problems since she is a most charming and cultured young woman and will doubtless prove an admirable companion for Peta during her spare time . . . .

"Well!" said Peta slowly, laying the letter down. She looked ruefully at her aunt. It seemed as if their peaceful existence was indeed to be rudely disrupted! Two guests—one of whom was apparently an elderly invalid and the other a "charming and cultured young woman"! It was difficult to say which would be worse!

Ann was still looking very much put out, like a broody hen which had had its feathers ruffled. It was just like her brother, she thought indignantly, to make his plans entirely to suit himself! He simply had no idea what a burden this huge house was . . . it was all she could do now to get the housework and gardening done. How could she possibly look after two guests as well as Peta and John?

She said distractedly, "I wonder if I'd be able to get Mrs. Brooks to come and give me a hand . . . I know she hasn't been well lately, but perhaps just for a short time. . . ."

"I'll help you, Ann." Peta's offer came instantaneously. She couldn't bear to see that worried look on Ann's face.

Ann laughed in spite of herself. "Oh, Peta, what about that job of yours? Besides, you know you loathe cooking and housework."

Peta grimaced. "I do know. But you can't cope with everything on your own. It's beastly unfair of Uncle John to expect you to! Why don't you tell him so?"

Ann sighed. "He just doesn't realise. I suppose I'll just have to try to manage. Except," she added grimly, "that I have no intention of trying to provide entertainment for Dr. Waring. That will have to be your job, I'm afraid, Peta."

She spoke with a certain amount of underlying relief. A shy, self-conscious woman, desperately reserved, she had always found it difficult to make friends or to talk freely to strangers. particularly those who were on the same intellectual level as her brilliant brother.

"I'm afraid I won't be much good." Peta's grin was a little rueful. "I don't think I'm the sort of person who appeals to elderly archaeologists!"

Ann looked at her anxiously, remembering one or two stormy scenes in the past.

"You and John have never really had a chance to get to know each other." She hesitated, then added with a rush, "I know that there may be—well, difficulties, but you will try to keep the peace this time, won't you, dear? John *is* difficult and a little intolerant at times, I admit that, but—I do so hate quarrels and unpleasantness and—and he's sure to blame me if. . . ." Her voice trailed away into nothing and she blinked nervously.

Peta flung her arms round her and hugged her.

"You mean that he's bound to blame you for my shortcomings, I suppose! All right, dearest, I'll be angelic! I'll even take his Miss Kent to my bosom for your sake—though I must say it doesn't sound as if she's exactly my type, does it?" she added, picking up the letter and reading it through again.

Ann's gaze rested on the downbent head. She was just beginning to realise that Peta was a curiously individual person, quite unlike most of her contemporaries. Too headstrong and too much of a tomboy, according to the Vicar's wife. Well, she'd always been headstrong and Ann had found it far easier to give way than to argue. Perhaps she ought to have been much stricter, but she couldn't really say that she had any passionate regrets. Peta, despite her wild ways, was basically a very much nicer and kinder person than either of the Vicar's conventionally brought up daughters!

Perhaps, she thought hopefully, looking as always for a silver lining, this girl who was coming to the house would have a good influence on Peta . . . persuade her to be a little less harum-scarum, a little more . . . feminine. At least John would approve of her more. She sighed involuntarily. Those two had never got on at all well, neither understood the other and they were both obstinate and had strong wills. But there the resemblance ended, for whereas Peta was warm-hearted and vulnerable, John cared for nothing and nobody but his work.

She sighed again and began to clear away the breakfast things. The sooner she set to work and got two extra bedrooms ready the better. The beds hadn't been slept in for ages, so they were almost bound to be damp, even though she did try to remember to put hot bottles in at regular intervals!

Peta went off to work, driving, as she always did, her aunt's small car. Ann had bought it years ago on a sudden impulse which she had later regretted, for when it came to the point she had been far too nervous to learn how to drive it. Now it was more or less Peta's property. After only a few lessons she had passed her driving test first time, and even Ann, who had been induced to accompany her on one or two rare occasions, was satisfied that she was a safe and careful driver. (She never took risks which might involve other people, that was something Mike had drummed into her.)

Thoughts of her guardian's letter haunted her all day, spoiling her usual enjoyment of her work. Normally her problems ceased to exist when she was sailing and she abandoned herself to joy like a bird to the wind, but today the magic was missing. Even Major Norwell, not the most observant of men, noticed that she'd lost what he jokingly called her "sparkle."

"Anything wrong, my dear?" he asked, genuine concern showing in his kind, ugly face. Both he and his wife Marjorie were fond of Peta and were glad of her enthusiastic participation in their venture. Getting the sailing school well established was a tricky business and the margin between success and failure very small.

Peta shook her head. The Norwells were kind, but she couldn't talk to them about her personal problems.

"Nothing. I'm probably just a bit tired," she said, and wisely Major Norwell accepted the excuse without further comment.

Silently Peta accused herself of being an idiot. She wasn't usually prone to meeting trouble halfway, but in this instance she felt that perhaps her apprehension was justified. Uncle John by himself would have been bad enough, but two total strangers as well. . . . ! Luckily the doctor man wasn't likely to present any major problems, probably he'd be quite happy to potter about in the garden and snooze in the sun, but what about Miss Kent? Of course she'd be working with Uncle John most of the time, but when she was off duty would she expect Peta to be her constant companion? It was a distinctly disturbing prospect.

It was obviously unwelcome, too, to Mike. Peta, telling him that evening about her guardian's letter, was not surprised to see his fair brows draw together in a startled frown.

"I don't suppose you and the allegedly charming young woman have a single thing in common! You should see the so-called secretaries in my office, all paint and mini-skirts! I doubt if they know one end of a boat from the other."

Peta smiled a little ruefully. "It's a nuisance, but I'll have to be nice to her, Mike. It's only fair."

"Well, please don't involve me!" Mike said curtly. "As far as I'm concerned two is company and three is none, and don't you forget it."

Peta shot him a quick glance. Mike had always been a little possessive in his attitude towards her and liking him as she did, she had never really minded, though sometimes she had found it puzzling. Her own instinct was to be friends with everyone, but she knew that Mike didn't feel this way and that he rather resented it because she did.

She said coaxingly, "Well, we could take her out in *Romany* sometimes, couldn't we? She'd probably enjoy that."

"I don't doubt it, but nothing doing. I don't want any chattering females on *my* boat!" Mike sounded almost aggressive, but his lips quirked into a reluctant grin as he saw the mischievous sparkle in Peta's tawny eyes. "Oh, all right, I know you're a female, but thank God you *don't* chatter."

Peta laughed. "I do sometimes. Ask Ann."

To her surprise Mike's face suddenly shadowed. He hesitated, then said rather awkwardly, "By the way, was she worried because you were so late home last night?"

Peta stared at him. "Worried? Of course not. Why

should she have been? She knew I was with you. I telephoned her before we had supper."

"Yes, I know, but. . . ." Mike stopped abruptly, as if suddenly changing his mind about what he had been going to say. Then, seeing the bewilderment on Peta's face, he reluctantly explained.

"Actually Mother was a bit het up. Said I'd got no business keeping you out till that time of night. Heaven knows why, unless she's afraid the old tabby-cats will start to talk."

"About *us*?" Peta's laugh pealed out and after a moment Mike joined in, relieved that she saw the funny side of it.

Peta sobered suddenly and regarded him a little anxiously.

"Was your mother really upset, Mike? Didn't you explain about the car?"

"Of course I did." Mike returned her look and then grinned. She didn't look a day older than his young sister at the moment, he thought, with her hair blown anyhow and her face shining, and it occurred to him that he couldn't remember the last time he had seen her in anything but a shirt and denim trews. Goodness only knew what his mother was worrying about!

He reached out his hand and gave her hair a friendly tweak.

"Forget it, old thing. It's of no importance. I just wondered if dear old Ann had been in a state too, that's all."

Later on Peta might have remembered that significant "too" and wondered, but there were other, more pressing things to occupy her mind. Her guardian's letter—which had taken several days to arrive—was followed by a surprise cable announcing that he would be catching an earlier plane than he had originally intended and would consequently arrive in England twenty-four hours sooner than he had stated in his letter. Since Ann was indulging in a bout of belated spring-cleaning this not unnaturally plunged her into a state of wild confusion.

"It's only him, apparently. That's one consolation."

26

Peta studied the cablegram carefully. "He doesn't mention the others, so I suppose they must be coming later. Would you like me to fetch him from the station, Ann? I'm pretty sure Major Norwell would give me some time off if I explained."

Ann shook her head.

"I think not, dear. I'd better order a taxi." She sighed. "I seem to remember that he hasn't got a very high opinion of women drivers. I know he was very cross when I bought the car, he said it was a complete waste of money and really I suppose he would have been quite right if *you* hadn't learned how to drive it!"

Peta smiled her gamine grin. "I won't meet him if you think it might be too much of a shock, but I can assure you that at some future date I intend to make him revise his ideas! Women quite often make better drivers than men, only they'll never admit it!"

"I don't suppose you'll change John's mind. But the car may come in useful, for Miss Kent and Dr. Waring, I mean."

"Yes, if the poor old chap has been ill he probably won't want to do much walking," Peta agreed. "Which bedroom are you giving him, Ann?"

"The one next to yours. I know it's rather small, but there's a good view from the window and it gets a nice lot of sun. I only hope he won't find our steep stairs too much for him," Ann said anxiously, for like Peta she had visions of an elderly, rather frail man who would probably require a certain amount of cosseting.

"And Miss Kent?"

"She's having my room. Yes!"—as Peta protested, "I can easily make do with the box room for a little while. If we have to have visitors foisted upon us I mean to make sure that they're reasonably comfortable, and Americans are used to such a high standard of living, I believe."

Peta looked puzzled. "Americans?"

"Well, I assume Miss Kent is an American. Your uncle engaged her in New York," Ann pointed out.

It was a reasonable assumption but hopelessly inaccurate, as they learned the next day when John Devlin

27

told them something of his new secretary's background.

"She is a delightful girl," he said in his dry, pedantic way. "Just as English as you and I, but very widely travelled. Her father was in the diplomatic service all his life and after her mother's death she kept house for him and acted as his secretary as well. They were in Peru for two years and Waring and I occasionally enjoyed their hospitality. A few months ago, however, Mr. Kent died and his daughter was left without home or family or very much money. It was Waring who suggested that I might offer her a job, and I'm glad that I did, for the poor child jumped at it. She badly wanted to return to England, and I for my part feel that I'm fortunate to have such an intelligent young woman to work for me."

"How old is she?" Peta was sitting cross-legged on the floor, her tawny hair falling over her face and hiding her expression.

"Not much more than twenty, I should imagine, but of course she has the poise of a far older woman. As I've said, she has travelled a good deal and done a lot of entertaining on her father's behalf."

Ann looked doubtful. "It sounds as though she's led a very busy and interesting life. Won't she find it rather quiet here?"

"Oh, she's the sort of girl who adapts very easily—gets on well with everyone," her brother assured her. "You'll like her, Ann, and Waring too. He's a brilliant archaeologist—done some splendid work in Peru, absolutely first-rate!"

This was not exactly what Ann and Peta most wanted to know about him, but evidently Professor Devlin did not feel disposed to volunteer any further information. Ann contented herself with one last vital question.

"When are they coming here?"

"Tomorrow. Waring is bringing Miss Kent down by car: I gather she's got a fair bit of luggage. If I'd waited I could have come with them myself, but I was anxious to get home. I've been away a long time."

He smiled at his sister and relaxed in the depths of

his armchair with a sigh of content. A wanderer for most of his life, his roots were in Norfolk and he always looked forward to returning "home". Nothing, he thought, ever seemed to change much during his absence. No doubt there were some new faces in the village, and some old friends missing, but otherwise it looked just the same. And this house, even this room, never altered, it was much as he remembered it as a boy. There were the same chairs and the same rugs, and the same Dresden china figures standing on the big old-fashioned mantelpiece, and though curtains and loose covers must have been replaced several times, they surely differed little from the originals! Ann, of course, was timeless, but Peta. . . . For the first time since his arrival he really looked at his ward, and at what he saw he frowned slightly.

Ann saw both the look and the critical frown and her heart missed a beat. She said quickly, "Peta dear, would you go and see if the kettle's boiling? A cup of coffee would be nice."

Peta rose willingly. Her guardian watched her cross the room, but there was no admiration in his eyes for the easy swing of her slender figure or for the proud carriage of her head. Instead, an expression of faint distaste crossed his narrow face.

"Except for her hair, that child looks more like a boy than a girl! When does she leave school, Ann?"

"She—she's left. She's got a job—teaching people how to sail," Ann said with a rush. She was not at all sure, now it came to the point, that her brother was going to approve of Peta's choice of career.

"*What*? She's left school? Already? My dear Ann——!"

"John! She's eighteen—nearly nineteen. She couldn't stay at school for ever!" Ann protested.

For a moment John Devlin looked aback. He had never been any good at remembering ages, and to him Peta certainly did not look much more than fifteen or sixteen. Then he recovered himself and his thin mouth tightened a little.

"Even if she's left school she should be at University

or undergoing some kind of training. In my absence it was up to you, Ann, to see that she chose a suitable career."

"I wanted her to do something she liked. At least she's happy," Ann said defensively.

"Stuff and nonsense! You spoil the child—always have!" John Devlin looked profoundly irritated and his eyes gleamed with a steely grey colour as they looked at her. "Teaching people how to sail, indeed! What kind of a job is that? I shall have to talk to her—talk to her seriously!"

"Yes, but not tonight!" Ann pleaded. "Not your first night home, John! Wait a day or two."

For a moment he hesitated, then he shrugged. "Very well. I should prefer to make my opinion known immediately, but it shall be as you wish." He spoke stiffly, and Ann read his disapprobation in his eyes. So, too, did Peta when she returned to the drawing room with the coffee, and at the first opportunity she cornered Ann.

"You've told him about the sailing school, haven't you? I thought so!" she said gloomily. "He looks positively blighting! Is he going to be difficult?"

"He may be. I should keep out of his way tomorrow," Ann shamelessly counselled. She dreaded the thought of open friction between her brother and his ward. Peta, she knew, would try to keep the peace for her sake, but she had a quick temper and could only be driven so far. "Once the others arrive he'll probably forget all about you and me. His book will occupy his mind to the complete exclusion of everything else."

"That's a thought!" Peta grinned at her in relief. "I've got a day off tomorrow, but Mike's racing at Horning: he asked me to crew for him, but I said I didn't think I could. I'll ring him up and ask him whether he still wants me or whether he's made other arrangements."

It was Mrs. Mandeville, and not Mike, who answered the telephone and their conversation was brief and to the point. No, Mike was not in and yes, she was quite sure he had made other arrangements for Saturday, he had asked Tommy Hayes to crew for him.

When she had said goodbye Peta put the receiver down very slowly and stood looking at it, a little crease growing between her arched eyebrows. Mrs. Mandeville had sounded practically like a stranger . . . distant, almost chilly! Of course the telephone often distorted people's voices, but even so . . . it was odd!

In the event she was glad that Mike's plans had already been made, for Major Norwell telephoned early next morning to ask if she could possibly forgo her day off. His wife was in bed with a devastating attack of migraine and it was impossible for him to manage without help.

Peta, assenting readily, left the house before her guardian was even up. She felt slightly guilty about leaving Ann to cope with everything, including the expected arrival of Dr. Waring and Miss Kent, but contented herself with the reflection that they probably wouldn't arrive much before six o'clock and she would be home herself by then. Ann had warned her not to be late: John Devlin made rather a fetish of punctuality, especially where meals were concerned.

It was a singularly cheerless day, grey and chilly, and it looked as though at any moment it might begin to rain. Two of Marjorie Norwell's pupils turned up, but the third cancelled his lesson at the last minute, and Peta, finding time on her hands, seized the opportunity to scrub down two of the dinghies. She was feeling curiously tense and strung up, and hard work made her feel a little better, though not much.

"Well done, my dear. No one could ever say you shirk the dirty jobs!" Stephen Norwell came up behind her as she rubbed at a porthole until she could see her face in it, and gave her an approving smile. He cast an experienced eye over the spotless decks, neatly coiled ropes and gleaming portholes, then glanced first at his watch and then at the river. Boats were coming in early tonight, mooring in rows, two or three deep, in the dykes and artificial harbours beside the main river. Holidaymakers did not like this sort of weather.

He laid his hand on Peta's shoulder. "You wouldn't

like to leave a few minutes early and look in on Marjorie on your way home, I suppose? I shan't be back until fairly late and she's been alone all day."

"Of course I will." A little surprised by the request, Peta gave a final polish to the last porthole and went to wash her hands and run a comb through her hair. She'd missed Marjorie today: her gaiety was usually infectious. Like her husband she worked very hard, and Peta hoped that she wasn't overdoing things. Just lately she had looked rather wan and there had been dark circles under her eyes.

The Norwells' small thatched cottage was at the far end of the village. Peta, driving with her customary care along the narrow lanes bordered by high hedges, honked angrily as the small van she was following suddenly swung into a side road without giving a signal.

"Heavens, that's the Allport boy . . . nobody with him and he's only just started to drive, he can't possibly have passed his test yet!" Peta frowned to herself and wondered if the boy's father knew what he was up to. He was probably past caring . . . Charlie was one of the wild ones, he'd been in and out of trouble all his life.

Then, abruptly, she forgot all about Charlie Allport. She was on the point of slowing down to take a nasty bend when a small black-and-white dog, appearing from nowhere, suddenly hurtled across the road right in front of her wheels. There was no time to think. Following a blind instinct she swerved violently and lurched on to the wrong side of the road just as a long, sleek car, travelling at speed, rounded the bend and came at her like a torpedo. She wrenched violently at the wheel, swayed crazily across the road and mounted the grass verge, almost deafened by the hideous screech of brakes and tyres as the other car came to a skidding halt.

The engine cut. Peta sat for a few seconds with her head bowed on to the driving wheel, almost unable to believe that she was alive and unharmed and that the car was the right way up. She felt sick and dizzy. A door slammed and she looked up to see the driver of the other car, a tall, dark man in a charcoal-grey suit, striding purposefully towards her, his face grim. He looked furiously angry.

"Are you all right?" The question came harshly, with an underlying anxiety which Peta was too discomposed to recognize. It did not occur to her that he was as shaken as she was and that this had made him angry.

Dumbly she nodded, then managed a wavering smile. "Yes, I think so."

She heard his breath expelled in a quick sigh of relief, but when he spoke his voice was low and furious.

"Then you're a damn sight luckier than you deserve to be! What the hell made you try to take that bend on the wrong side of the road? You came bloody near being killed!" His eyes narrowed suspiciously. "How old are you? Have you got a licence?"

A wave of crimson swept across Peta's white face. She was not used to being sworn at. "Of course I have! It—it wasn't my fault I was on the wrong side of the road! A dog ran out in front of me and I had to swerve or I would have hit it!"

"I didn't see a dog."

Peta's eyes blazed. "Are you accusing me of being a liar?"

"No, but it does occur to me that someone in your position might well find it expedient to invent an excuse for what actually amounts to downright bad driving," he said grimly. "Dog or no dog, the fact remains that you might have killed yourself and two other people into the bargain!"

For the first time Peta became aware that there was a passenger in the front seat of the Mercedes-Benz. She had a vague impression of a lovely, flower-like face framed by a mass of spun-gold hair, then she dragged her attention back to the man.

"Come to that, you're not such a marvellous driver yourself!" she snapped. "You came round that bend miles too fast and that beastly big car of yours hogs all the road, it doesn't give anyone else a chance!"

It was a completely illogical attack and she knew it, but there was a slight pause during which she had the impression he was somewhat taken aback. Then he said, in a voice in which there was now, incredibly, a note of faint amusement, "You do believe in taking the war into the enemy's camp, don't you?"

The girl in the Mercedes-Benz wound down her window and stuck out her head.

"Nick, for heaven's sake hurry up! We're blocking the road!" Her voice was distinctive, clear and beautiful, but it held a note of obvious impatience.

For a moment the man hesitated, but a loud honking from a lorry which had pulled up behind the Mercedes-Benz confirmed the girl's words.

"Right! I'm coming!" he called back. Then, to Peta, "If you were my daughter I wouldn't trust you out on a fairy cycle! Take a bit more care in future—the next time you try to round a bend on the wrong side of the road you may not be so lucky!"

With this parting shot he turned on his heel and went back to his own car, his stride swift and sure. Peta, watching him, thought angrily that she had never seen a more arrogant carriage. Detestable man! She was conscious, as the Mercedes roared past her, that she was trembling, but with rage rather than from shock. How *dared* he speak to her like that, as if she were some kind of juvenile delinquent? Oh, he'd had a right to be angry, there had nearly been an extremely nasty accident, but he'd so patently disbelieved her about the dog and some of his remarks had been downright insulting!

One consolation, she was hardly likely to see him again. He was a visitor, of course: one didn't have to be a Sherlock Holmes to deduce that, but he didn't look the type to "rough it" on the Broads. Nor, come to that, did his beautiful passenger! His wife, perhaps? Peta remembered the half amused, half bored expression she'd seen on the girl's lovely face, and writhed inwardly. However good her excuse, she'd been hopelessly in the wrong and she'd had the fact well and truly rubbed in! It was not, she thought wryly, an experience that she would like to have repeated!

She took a deep breath, let in the clutch, and eased

the car slowly off the verge, which at this point was a muddy grass bank, mercifully not very steep. Luckily nothing seemed to have been damaged, but she was still feeling a little shaky and she was glad when she reached the Norwell's cottage. Marjorie, who was curled up in a deep comfortable armchair, greeted her warmly and seemed to notice nothing amiss.

"I feel an absolute fraud!" she said ruefully. "My head is tons better, but I knew that if I turned up at the School this afternoon Stephen would blow his top and send me straight home again."

Only a year or two younger than her husband, who was in his late thirties, Marjorie Norwell was a rosy brunette with a bubbling personality and a delightful smile. Just at the moment she looked pale and washed-out, but though the effervescence was missing it had been replaced by a sweet, secret glow which Peta found rather puzzling.

"I'm glad you're better: your husband seemed worried about you. He won't be back until late so he asked me to call in case there was something you needed," she explained.

Marjorie's expression was one of dismay. "Oh dear, I do hope he isn't going to fuss like this for the next seven months!" She grinned at Peta's startled face. "He hasn't told you, then? I'm going to have a baby, Peta: the doctor confirmed it last night. I've been feeling a bit out of sorts for weeks, but never dreamed it could be that!"

Peta stared at her. This was a development she had never even contemplated! "A *baby*? Oh, Mrs. Norwell, how aw—I m-mean, what about the School?" she blurted out.

"You mean my timing isn't exactly fortuitous?" Marjorie asked wryly. "No, I suppose it isn't, but we'll manage somehow. When you've waited for a baby for as long as Stephen and I have, Peta, nothing else seems to matter!"

"Mmmm." Peta sounded dubious. She couldn't help thinking that it was a great pity that the baby hadn't waited until the sailing school was well and truly established! Marjorie, reading her thoughts aright, laughed.

"You're an odd child, Peta! Don't you want to get married and have babies one day? Most girls do."

"Well, I'm not most girls!" Peta said decidedly. "I want to be free. Besides"—with a grin—"I don't suppose I shall ever meet anyone I'd like to marry!"

"What about——" Marjorie began teasingly, then stopped short. She and Stephen did not altogether care for Mike Mandeville, though they knew him well. He was an attractive young man but he had, they agreed, few sensitivies.

Peta didn't notice the pause. She had gone into the neat little kitchen to make coffee and sandwiches, but when this was done she refused Marjorie's invitation to stay and talk. It was almost six o'clock and she knew that if she wasn't home in time for the evening meal there would be unpleasant repercussions. There was no need to antagonise her guardian unnecessarily!

By the time she left the cottage the rain, which had held off all day, was coming down quite fast. She made a dash for the car, but she had not driven more than a few yards down the lane when an ominous bump-bump made her stop and investigate. One tyre was as flat as a pancake! She must have punctured it when she'd mounted the verge.

Stifling a groan—this certainly wasn't her lucky day—she abandoned all hope of getting home in time for dinner and set to work to change the wheel. When she had at last finished she was soaked to the skin, and what was even worse it was well after half-past six when she swung the car into Greylings' driveway. There was no sign of another car: perhaps, she thought hopefully, Dr. Waring had not yet arrived. Of course, he might have parked his car behind the house, but there simply wasn't time to find out.

Stealthily she let herself into the house, hoping to creep up into her room and divest herself of her wet clothing before anyone realised she was back. She could hear the rise and fall of voices in the drawing-room: evidently Dr. Waring and Miss Kent *had* arrived but they hadn't yet started dinner. She could hear Ann moving about in the kitchen. She began to tiptoe swiftly across the hall, but in her haste she caught her toe in a large, fringed rug and despite her frantic efforts to save herself she sprawled headlong. The umbrella stand fell over with a loud clatter and as she picked herself up, ruefully rubbing a bruised elbow, the door of the sitting room swung open. Her guardian stood looking at her, his face registering surprise and displeasure, and there behind him was a tall, dark-haired man whose face and bearing were odiously familiar. The driver of the Mercedes-Benz!

Peta, forgetting all about her sore elbow, gave a gasp of sheer horror.

"You!" she said in a voice pregnant with loathing, and she stood stock-still, staring at him with eyes that were wide with dismay and disbelief.

CHAPTER THREE

THE man's well-cut lips twitched, she could have sworn with amusement.

"Good evening," he said pleasantly, and it almost seemed as though his eyes flashed her a warning.

Baffled, Professor Devlin looked from one to the other. "Peta, this is Dr. Waring. You surely haven't already met?"

Peta was still rooted to the spot and she hardly heard him.

"I—I thought you'd be *old*!" she stammered, and there was an almost accusing note in her voice. How could she *possibly* have known that that arrogant stranger was Dr. Nicholas Waring? Anyone less like the conventional idea of an archaeologist could hardly be imagined! Tall, dark and handsome . . . inevitably the ridiculous cliché repeated itself in her mind and she had to suppress a wild desire to giggle hysterically.

Nicholas Waring raised his dark brows. "You did? I am sorry, in that case, to disappoint you." His amusement was now perfectly apparent and Peta found herself flushing hotly at her own gaucherie.

"Peta!" That was her guardian's voice, sharp with annoyance, but before he could say anything further another figure emerged from the drawing room. Slender, golden, she stood with one hand resting lightly on Nicholas Waring's arm, her green eyes wide with surprise.

"Good heavens! The girl on the wrong side of the road!" Her voice was even lovelier than Peta remembered—full, and a little deeper than the ordinary, with the tone of a beautiful muffled bell in it.

Instant comprehension dawned in Professor Devlin's deep set eyes and his sallow face flushed.

"I can hardly believe . . . surely my ward is not the girl you've just been telling me about, Miss Kent? The one who almost caused a serious accident?"

There was a moment's embarrassed silence which

38

spoke for itself. John Devlin, his lips compressed to a thin, bloodless line, turned to Peta.

"Upon my word, Peta, I'm ashamed of you! You're obviously quite unfit to drive a car at all! From all accounts you very nearly killed yourself and two innocent people into the bargain!"

"It wasn't entirely her fault, as Loriol should have told you." Nicholas Waring spoke quickly. "She had to swerve to avoid hitting a dog."

His gaze fixed itself on the ceiling and he added lightly, "In any case I *was* travelling rather fast and my car does—er—hog quite a lot of the road!"

Peta's eyes flashed. Now he was adding insult to injury by making fun of her! She swept him a withering look, then, standing defiantly erect, she looked her guardian straight in the eye and spoke very clearly.

"Dr. Waring is quite aware that what happened was entirely my fault, Uncle. I don't believe I apologised at the time for the inconvenience I caused him, but naturally I'm extremely sorry. And now, if you'll excuse me, I'll go and change. I'm rather wet."

"And very late!" Her guardian, following her to the foot of the stairs, snapped out the words. "We've been waiting dinner for you for half an hour!" He looked her up and down and Peta suddenly became acutely conscious not only of her wet, clinging shirt and jeans but also of her dishevelled hair and grimy hands. "What on earth have you been doing to get yourself into such a disgraceful condition?"

Peta went very white. Did he have to humiliate her like this, in public?

"My tyre was flat. I had to change it," she said unsteadily.

"Well, hurry up and make yourself presentable! And Peta! Despite your extraordinary preference for boy's attire, I should be obliged if you would find either a skirt or a dress in your wardrobe! That much courtesy, at least, is owed to our guests!"

Professor Devlin, now thoroughly heated, did not bother to lower his voice and his words must have been clearly audible to Nicholas Waring and the girl he had called Loriol, though neither was still in the hall.

Peta gasped. Then, choking back the hot, angry words that rose to her lips, she turned and fled up the stairs and into the refuge of her own tiny room. Quivering with resentment and hurt pride, she flung herself full length on her bed, biting her lips to keep back her tears. She felt shocked and bewildered. How *could* he have spoken to her like that, in front of strangers? Well, at least it had doubtless provided that destestable Dr. Waring with an additional source of amusement!

The thought of facing him and Loriol Kent, after that crushing humiliation, was almost more than she could bear. For one wild moment she considered the possibility of locking her door and not appearing for dinner at all, but apart from the fact that that would worry Ann, she wasn't going to run away from anything! That was a coward's way out!

Pride flooded back hotly into her veins, stiffening her spine, and she jumped up. Hastily she tore off her wet clothes, leaving them in a bedraggled little heap on the floor. Next she washed her hands and then her face—that was streaked with dirt and grease as well, what a sketch she must have looked when she came in!—and brushed her hair. Then she hesitated. She saw no reason why her guardian should dictate to her about her clothes, but she knew quite well that if she appeared at the table wearing trews and a shirt he was quite capable, in his present mood, of ordering her to go and change. If it weren't for poor Ann . . . and the presence of strangers . . . she'd risk a showdown, but not tonight!

She crossed slowly to her wardrobe and looked gloomily inside. Somewhere there should be the navy blue serge skirt she'd worn in the Sixth at school. That would do—or so she thought until she eventually found it. It had fallen off its hanger and was lying in a creased and crumpled heap at the bottom of the wardrobe. Impossible to wear it until it had been pressed!

Stifling a groan, Peta searched feverishly for an alternative. There was only one, a dress that Ann had chosen for her two years ago, and which she had hardly worn. It was an unbecoming colour and the style was impossibly juvenile—little puffed sleeves, embroidery on the bodice, and a Peter Pan collar—but there was nothing else. She put it on, then stood staring into her mirror. She looked about twelve! If she *looked* like a child, how could she expect anyone to treat her as a grown-up?

Savagely she pulled open the drawer of her dressing table. Some well-meaning person had given her some cosmetics last Christmas and up to now she'd never felt the slightest desire to use them. She'd never worn lipstick in her life, but tonight she had to do *something* to restore her morale! Uncertainly she began to investigate the contents of the little blue box which she unearthed from the back of the drawer. Eye-shadow—she wasn't going to experiment with that! Powder—that was easy, all you had to do was to pat it on. Lipstick . . . what an odd colour! Peta eyed it disapprovingly, then, taking a deep breath, leaned forward and applied it to her lips. It was hard not to smear it and she wasn't absolutely sure whether it was an improvement or not, but it *must* make her look older!

Defiantly she shut the box. For a few moments longer she lingered, then, head held high, she went slowly down the stairs to join the others.

They had already started their meal. Everyone looked up as she came through the door and she saw at once that there was anxiety and apprehension in Ann's face. Poor dear, she was afraid of Uncle John! She gave her a quick, would-be reassuring smile and with a murmured apology for her lateness, sat down in her place.

"Hurry up with your soup, Peta, you'll catch us up." John Devlin's voice was cold and colourless, but at least he made no remarks about her appearance. The conversation, which had ceased when she came in, started up again and Peta, left alone to eat her consommé, glanced covertly round the table.

Loriol Kent was seated next to the Professor. Looking at her, Peta realised for the first time the full force of her beauty. Wonderful shining hair . . . brilliant green eyes . . . exquisite features . . . Good heavens, thought Peta in genuine admiration, she's absolutely wasted as a

41

secretary, she ought to be a model or a film star! No wonder even her stiff, dessicated guardian had succumbed to her charms!

She felt no resentment because it was Loriol who had given her away to her guardian. It hadn't been intentional: she'd been startled and she'd spoken on the spur of the moment. No, she reserved all her animosity for Nicholas Waring, for even if he *had* made a half-hearted attempt to defend her, he'd already shown quite clearly that he was thoroughly enjoying her discomfiture!

He was sitting opposite, and though Peta found it impossible to look at him without feeling dislike and antagonism, she had to admit that physically, at least, he had a certain attraction. His eyes were woodsmoke grey under heavy black eyebrows and—surprisingly— they were scored at their corners with unmistakable laughter lines. The lean face with its high cheekbones was deeply tanned and his lips were sharply defined and held firm at the corners. Although he was sitting very still and his expression was inscrutable, he conveyed an almost overwhelming impression of easy, controlled strength . . . of a subtle, dynamic force. So much for her imaginary picture of a frail, pale invalid!

Perhaps he felt her gaze, for he turned his head and his eyes met hers. Maddeningly, green fire danced and laughed in their smoky depths, even though his firm lips were gravely unsmiling. Covered with inexplicable confusion, Peta swallowed a spoonful of consommé a little too quickly and choked violently. Damn the man! she thought furiously. How she wished she could tell him exactly what she thought about him!

Deliberately, before he could speak, she concentrated her attention on what the Professor was telling his secretary. Something extraordinarily interesting, judging from her absorbed expression! Under the screen of her thick, gold-tipped lashes Peta watched them both, amazed at her guardian's animation and wondering anew what had brought a girl as lovely as Loriol Kent to this remote Norfolk village. Surely she could have had her pick of exciting, glamorous jobs? Why, then, had she chosen to help an elderly, not very attractive professor to write what would probably be a very dull book?

Almost as though she read her thoughts Loriol smiled at her across the table, her green eyes wide and guileless.

"Don't you find archaeology absolutely fascinating, Peta? I do think you're lucky, having someone like Professor Devlin for your guardian! You must have learned an awful lot from him."

Peta again went scarlet. In actual fact she found archaeology incredibly boring and she had never made any secret of that fact.

"I'm afraid," John Devlin said in his dry way, "you are quite mistaken, Miss Kent. Peta has never evinced the slightest interest in my work and I very much doubt whether she has ever visited a museum in her life. Am I not right, my dear?"

There was a sarcastic inflection in his voice which stung. Peta lifted her head and looked at him steadily.

"Perfectly, Uncle. I can't see much point in delving into the past and I find antiquities very dull."

Loriol gave a quick reproachful exclamation and Professor Devlin's brows rushed together. Before he could answer, however, Nicholas Waring's deep, unhurried voice cut in.

"What are your interests, then, Peta?"

"She loves sailing." Ann, who had been listening apprehensively, threw him a grateful glance and, since Peta was slow to reply, answered for her. "Have—you ever done any, Dr. Waring?"

He shook his head, smiling slightly. "I'm afraid not, but I suppose that if one lives on or near the Broads the natural instinct is to gravitate towards a boat?"

"Not really," Peta answered coolly. "The opportunity is there, but the incentive is often missing."

"I'd simply love to learn to sail!" Loriol turned eagerly to Nicholas, her eyes sparkling. "Nick, we both ought to try! Don't you think it would be fun? It's not difficult, is it, Peta?"

"Not at all."

"I'm afraid you must count me out." Nicholas

sounded politely regretful. "I really don't think I have much affinity with water."

That didn't surprise Peta, whose lip curled scornfully. Loriol, however, pouted deliciously, looking so disappointed that Professor Devlin smiled and patted her shoulder paternally. He's far nicer to her than he's ever been to me, Peta thought suddenly, and then told herself that she was being stupid.

"You must get Peta to give you a few lessons, my dear. That, at least, I believe she *is* qualified to do," he added, and again the sarcastic inflection was back in his voice.

Loriol looked at Peta, noticeably less enthusiastic. "Do you have your own boat?"

"No. I sail with a friend," Peta said briefly.

Loriol smiled winningly. "But there'd be room for me sometimes?"

Remembering Mike's ultimatum, Peta felt cornered. "Perhaps. I—I don't know. Mike's not very keen on beginners."

"Oh!" Loriol raised her delicately arched brows. "Well, of course, in that case. . . ."

Professor Devlin interposed, "I understand that my ward teaches at a local sailing school, Miss Kent. Perhaps she is reluctant to defraud her employers of a possible pupil!"

"Gracious, have you left school?" Loriol's eyes were as wide and guileless as before. "You looked such an infant when we first saw you, Peta. Nicholas was quite sure that you hadn't got a driving licence!"

Nicholas Waring made an involuntary movement which Peta did not see. Why, I believe she said that on purpose, she thought, almost stunned with surprise. She saw her guardian's face darken and his nostrils indent sharply, and said hotly, "I passed my test first time! *And* I didn't have to show anyone my birth certificate!"

"Oh, I'm sorry. I didn't mean. . . ." Loriol began, so sweetly apologetic that Peta wondered if she had misjudged her.

Before she could make up her mind Nicholas said

smoothly, "It's always fatal to guess at a woman's age. Do you remember that tribe of Indians we ran across in the jungle last year, Professor? There was one incredibly wizened old crone whom I took to be the tribal matriarch, though it subsequently transpired she wasn't yet forty! Luckily she was an exception—most of the women were pretty, though wild and shy."

He turned to Ann to answer a diffident question and the dangerous moment had passed. Even so Peta remained very much on the defensive, sitting straight and stiff on her carved Queen Anne chair and carefully avoiding looking at or speaking to Nicholas Waring. Not only had she lost her normal healthy appetite, she felt as though there was practically no air in the room and that its heavy atmosphere was pressing upon her like an actual physical weight. She answered any remarks made to her as briefly as possible, and since Ann was never talkative the conversation gradually became a three-cornered one, with Peru as the chief topic of discussion.

What Peta knew about that particular country would probably not have covered the back of a postage stamp, but she found herself listening with a greater interest than she would have believed possible. Her guardian was incapable of breathing life into his precise, pedantic sentences, but Nicholas had a gift, which even she grudgingly recognised, for painting vivid word-pictures in a few unforgettable phrases. Loriol, too, was a delightful conversationalist and Peta very soon realised two things. One, that the Professor's new secretary was as intelligent as she was beautiful and two, that there was a close and long-standing friendship between her and Nicholas. Time and again one or the other made a casual reference to a shared experience, and there was also a liberal sprinkling of 'Do you remembers?' on Loriol's part, though not on Nicholas'.

Peta couldn't help thinking that even if her guardian's association with the Ambassador and his daughter had been limited to an occasional dinner at their house, it was perfectly obvious that the same could not be said for his junior colleague. She found herself remembering that her guardian had said that it was Nicholas who had asked him to give Loriol a job—though of course he could hardly have done that had she not been qualified to do the work, and there did not seem to be very much doubt about that.

All in all she was devoutly thankful when the meal had ended and she was able to escape into the kitchen to help with the washing up. Later, at Ann's request, she took in the coffee, and found Loriol playing chess with her guardian. Nicholas, who was looking out of the window, came over and took the tray from her hands and subconsciously she noted his lightness of foot and perfect muscular control. Whatever he did he did with a lean and easy grace which, illogically, she resented.

"Do you play chess?"

"No." She answered him curtly and in order to avoid further conversation assumed an interest in the chess game which she did not actually feel. Although the Professor was something of an expert Loriol was by no means at a disadvantage, and made several brilliant moves which made her opponent give a whistle of appreciation.

She said, with a smiling glance at Nicholas, "I used to play a lot with my father. Bridge, too, when we got the chance. Perhaps we could have a game one night, if Peta would make a fourth?"

"Sorry. I have few social accomplishments." Peta spoke with her usual abrupt truthfulness and was not surprised when her guardian snorted. She thought with a sudden sense of desolation, 'He ought to have had a ward like Loriol . . . someone he could be really proud of!' She was so pretty and graceful and intelligent, and she was clever about clothes, too, for the green dress she was wearing was very simple and yet it enhanced the unusual colour of her eyes and looked distinctively right.

Peta sighed, and glanced round the room. To her surprise Ann, instead of retiring into a corner with her sewing basket, was talking quietly to Nicholas. Normally she was too shy to converse with people she did not know well, but she looked more relaxed in Nicholas

Waring's company than Peta had seen her for a long time. Like Loriol and the Professor they seemed quite oblivious of anyone but themselves, and Peta suddenly had a strange feeling of being shut out . . . unwanted. She slipped quietly from the room, and felt with an almost bitter certainty that no one was likely to miss her presence.

It annoyed and puzzled her that she minded. Wasn't that exactly what she wanted—to be free to do what she pleased? She was tired, she told herself: it had been a ghastly evening so far. A wave of despondency swept over her. She'd meant to try so hard to avoid any kind of conflict with her guardian, yet already he was seriously displeased with her and once or twice her own anger and resentment had been perilously near escaping from her control. She simply wasn't used to being ordered about like a child or having her actions questioned! At one time, reluctantly, she had obeyed her guardian's edicts, but things were different now, sooner or later he would simply have to accept the fact that during the last three years she had grown up.

As for Nicholas Waring . . . ! She still hadn't got over the shock of meeting him face to face for the second time! She remembered, with a tight feeling of impotent rage at the back of her throat, the little laughing light that she had seen dancing far back in his grey eyes. Hateful, odious man! The less she saw of him the better, though it might be difficult, living in the same house. She'd find it hard to avoid him completely. Or Loriol. She frowned to herself, for she did not like Loriol either and she wasn't sure why. She hoped it wasn't anything as petty as jealousy, but the fact remained that she couldn't think about lovely, golden Loriol without some confusion of feeling. She'd need a little longer to make up her mind. On the surface she appeared charming, honey-sweet, but. . . .

She sighed, and gave herself a little mental shake, dismissing the small cloud of uneasiness which had risen up in her mind. She went into the kitchen and helped herself to a glass of water, then came out again into the hall and stood wondering what to do with the rest of

47

the evening. She longed to go out for a walk and feel the cool air on her flushed cheeks, but it was still raining very hard, it was practically a downpour.

She would telephone Mike and perhaps he would come over to see her. He would be back from Horning by now. Her face brightened at the thought and she went eagerly to the telephone. Suddenly she found herself longing for the reassurance of Mike's friendly presence. Just at the moment she felt as though she hadn't got a single ally except Ann. . . . and even Ann seemed momentarily to have deserted her!

She lifted the receiver and dialled the number, hoping against hope that it would not be Mrs. Mandeville who answered. Her luck was in and it was Mike.

"Hello! Peta here. How did you get on this afternoon?"

"Rotten." There was no mistaking the gloom in Mike's voice: he sounded almost sullen. "We lost, and thanks to that ham-handed idiot Tom we also split a sail! I told the fool to take in a reef, but by the time he'd argued the toss the damage was done!"

"Oh, Mike! I'm sorry!" Peta had an immediate vision of a tattered sail threshing and snapping in a wild wind and knew how annoyed Mike must have been.

"Not half as sorry as I am. If there's one thing I loathe it's being made to look like a ruddy amateur!"

Peta hesitated. Then she said, "It seems to have been an unlucky day for both of us."

"You had trouble too? Pity you couldn't have crewed for me, old girl, you're worth three of Tommy Hayes! D'you know, he had the nerve to tell me I should have renewed the canvas long ago? Anyone would have thought it was *my* fault we had to sail in with the jib in rags!" Mike's voice was bitter: he was obviously labouring under a strong sense of grievance.

From behind the door of the drawing room came the sound of laughter. When had she heard quiet, shy Ann laugh like that before?

She said quickly, almost desperately, "Mike, can you come over? I—I'd rather like to see you."

"What, now? Sorry, old dear, can't be done. I've got

to do something about getting some new canvas. I thought I'd go over to Potter and see Billy Hope: he'll probably let me have what I want fairly cheaply. Finances are a bit low at the moment, unfortunately."

"Couldn't you wait until tomorrow?" The question was on the tip of Peta's tongue, but she bit it back. She had no right to expect Mike to be at her beck and call and he had no way of knowing how much, just at the moment, she wanted to see him.

Forlornly she replaced the receiver and went slowly upstairs to her room. Mike might have *asked* if there was anything the matter, she thought, then was immediately annoyed with herself for being unreasonable. Mike had always been single-minded: she'd known and accepted that from the beginning of their friendship.

Peta's room was one of the smallest of the bedrooms at Greylings, but she had chosen it because of the view. Standing at her window she could see right over the flat marshes to the shining ribbon of the river, and this more than compensated her for the fact that there was not much space for her possessions. Not that she had many: she did not like to be 'cluttered'. A small picture on the wall by her bed, some treasured books in a small bookcase, a radio and a record player and a few carefully-chosen records made up the sum total.

It was to the radio, now, that she turned. She switched it on and the sound of music filled the room. Debussy's 'Clair de Lune'. She slipped on to the floor and sat listening, her chin cupped in her hands. Her guardian had once said, with heavy sarcasm, that a slight and very elementary appreciation of music was the only trace of culture he could find in his ward, but though she loved Debussy and Tchaikovsky—whose 'Pathétique' followed—tonight she was unable to lose herself completely. Her thoughts were too tumultuous, her spirit too restless, and she could not stay still long enough to hear the end of the concert.

When she went downstairs again Ann was in the kitchen, preparing grapefruit for the following morning. She looked up, her expression relieved, as Peta walked in.

"Oh, there you are, dear! Feeling any better now?"

"Better?" Peta stared at her. "There hasn't been anything wrong with me!"

Ann hesitated, annoyed with herself for her lack of tact. Then, seeing the heavy frown on Peta's face, she said quietly, "Well, you weren't very amiable at dinner, were you, dear? Perhaps you were feeling shy. I was myself—until I realised that there was absolutely no need to be. Dr. Waring is such a charming man and Miss Kent, too, is so sweet and nice: I must say I'm agreeably surprised."

Fancy Ann speaking with such enthusiasm, Peta thought. Aloud she said incredulously, "You really mean you *like* Nicholas Waring? I think he's utterly destestable!"

Ann went slightly pink, but when she spoke it was with unaccustomed firmness.

"Yes, I do like him very much indeed. I really think you're being rather silly about him, Peta dear, and if you continue to show your dislike as plainly as you did tonight you'll only end up by badly upsetting your uncle. Which reminds me, perhaps you'd better go and say goodnight to him. He's in the library, but he's going to bed quite soon."

"I hope he won't want to read the Riot Act again!" Peta kicked savagely at the leg of a chair, the childish act of aggression somehow relieving her feelings. "Is he alone?"

"I think so. Miss Kent has gone up to her room, to finish her unpacking, and I believe Dr. Waring has gone up, too." Ann looked at her anxiously. "I don't think John will say anything to you tonight, dear. He's looking very tired: you know he finds the Norfolk air rather too strong for him just at first."

She was wrong, for Professor Devlin, finding himself alone with his ward for the first time, could not resist making a few stringent remarks both about her bad driving and her general behaviour. Peta, inwardly boiling, bore his strictures in tight-lipped silence, but when he had finished she rushed headlong out of the house, feeling that unless she escaped she would explode.

It had stopped raining, and the air, though cold and damp, was also fresh and sweet-smelling. She walked quickly down the drive as far as the gate at the bottom and stood leaning against it for a few moments, struggling to contain her indignation. Everywhere there was a silvered stillness, a silence which was broken, at last, by the sound of a footstep behind her.

She spun round and found herself facing Nicholas Waring. He looked taller than ever in the moonlight and the suggestion of hardness about his mouth and square chin was accentuated. His steady, ironic gaze was hard to interpret.

"What do you want?" Taken unawares, she spoke almost accusingly, and his dark brows lifted.

"Why, nothing. Like you, I am merely admiring the moonlight. A taste for nocturnal prowling appears to be something, at least, which we have in common."

She said coldly, "I was just going back to the house. Goodnight, Dr. Waring."

She would have slipped past him, but he barred her way.

"To listen to Debussy?" he asked coolly, and then, as she looked startled, "You forget my room is next to yours. I heard 'Claire de Lune' as I passed the door."

She eyed him with hostility.

"I suppose you've already complained that I make too much noise!"

His lips twitched. "On the contrary. I enjoy Debussy, though I must admit that I'd have thought that Wagner—something like the 'Ride of the Valkyries', for instance—would have been more to your taste."

He laughed at her expression. "Oh, pax, Peta! I know we made an unfortunate start, but can't we be friends? You have the most terrifying scowl, you know: it quite intimidated me at dinner!"

He's making fun of me again, she thought indignantly, and had no doubt that as before there was a little laughing light dancing far back in his eyes.

She answered without giving herself time to think, "I don't feel friendly towards you!"

"So I've noticed," he said mockingly, then became suddenly serious.

"Peta, will you believe me when I say that for all the tea in China I wouldn't have had the Professor know the circumstances under which we·first met? You must realise that Loriol and I had absolutely no idea who you were, and I really am extremely sorry that as a result of a few incautious words you were—well, hauled over the coals. It couldn't have been pleasant, especially in front of strangers."

The kindness in his voice was unexpected and oddly disconcerting. Too proud to accept sympathy, she flared up at once.

"You can spare me your commiseration, Dr. Waring! If it hadn't been that I expect it would have been something else!"

"Yes, I've noticed that you're at loggerheads." He paused, then added drily, "No doubt there are faults on both sides, but you don't exactly go out of your way to be conciliatory, do you?"

Peta flushed. All her old resentment came flooding back and she said hotly, "What's it to do with you?"

"Absolutely nothing." He regarded her thoughtfully. "How old are you, Peta? Seventeen? Eighteen?" Then, as she did not answer, "Whatever you are, you're very young for your age. Only someone very immature would think and behave as you do. Why don't you try growing up a bit? It can be fun, you know."

She stared at him incredulously as he searched in his pocket for a cigarette, and did not realise until a long time afterwards that it was his air of cool detachment which infuriated her even more than his words.

"Any more gratuitious advice, or may I go?" In spite of herself her voice shook.

He grinned suddenly and looked younger. "Only one thing more." Before she realised what he meant to do he took her chin in his fingers and gently tilted back her head. His eyes were light-filled and dancing.

"You have an enchanting face. It's a pity to spoil it with too much of the wrong make-up, very badly applied!"

"Oh!" Peta gasped, and jerked herself away, her face crimson, as light footsteps sounded behind them. Loriol's clear voice said, "So here you are, Nicholas! I've been looking for you everywhere!"

She looked from Nicholas to Peta, and her eyebrows rose very slightly. Her expression, for one fleeting unguarded moment, was nakedly revealing, but Peta, angry, confused and embarrassed, did not wait to hear what she had to say. With a mumbled 'Goodnight' she pushed past her and began walking swiftly up the drive and back to the house.

Behind her she heard the sound of Loriol's soft laugh and instinctively she looked back. The elder girl, her golden hair silvered in the moonlight, had moved very close to Nicholas and her lovely face was raised provocatively to his. Inexperienced, even naïve, though she was, Peta suddenly knew one thing with blinding certainty. Whatever had brought Loriol Kent to Norfolk it was not a desire to help John Devlin with his book. She had come simply and solely because of Nicholas Waring.

CHAPTER FOUR

DESPITE Peta's fears, Nicholas and Loriol made very little difference to the even tenor of life at Greylings. In fact, the days passed swiftly and uneventfully, with none of the wrangling and arguments that usually marred John Devlin's homecoming. As his sister had confidently predicted, he very quickly became almost totally immersed in his book. He was an exacting taskmaster and the hours he insisted on his secretary working were unusual: he liked to dictate to her in the evenings and to keep his days free for sorting through his notes and further research. Luckily Loriol did not seem to object to the arrangement. In fact she appeared to be tireless, and although the Professor dictated to her for hours on end she never failed to produce, at the end of each morning, a thick wad of typescript covering the dictation of the previous night. Nicholas, too, was caught up in the feverish activity and Ann sometimes wondered if her brother realised that far from enjoying a peaceful convalescence, the younger man, like Loriol, had very few leisure moments.

She said as much to Peta, whose retort was predictable.

"As far as I'm concerned I'm thankful for small mercies! The less I see of him the better I'm pleased!"

Ann sighed. Peta could be so unreasonable at times! She said gently, "You haven't seen very much of any of us just lately. You seem to be working very hard yourself. Have you got an extra lot of pupils?"

"Not really. It's Mrs. Norwell." Peta's face shadowed. "She isn't at all well, the baby that's on the way is wearing her out. She does her best to carry on as usual, but she simply has to give in sometimes and go home to bed. I know Major Norwell is worried about her, and about the School too, come to that, though he tries to hide it. I just feel that it's up to me to do everything I possibly can to help."

She looked at Ann and grinned. "Luckily Uncle

seems to have forgotten how much he disapproves of my choice of career! I only hope nobody will say anything to remind him!"

In actual fact she saw very little of her guardian, or of Nicholas and Loriol, except at dinner. This was an ordeal she could not avoid, though she always took good care to make her escape as soon as possible afterwards. Mike was a far more congenial companion or, when he was not available, Richard Mayne. Surprisingly, she and the artist had become firm friends. She was conscious of the fact that he enjoyed her company, though often when they were together she surprised a hint of wistfulness in his grey eyes which she found hard to understand. He was still in the process of painting her portrait, though she secretly thought he was wasting his time. Why did he want to paint someone whose mirror plainly told her that she was red-haired and skinny and freckled? If she were beautiful, like Loriol Kent, she could have understood his enthusiasm, for surely no artist would be able to look at that lovely face without wanting to paint it!

She sighed a little at the thought. She had definitely come to the conclusion that she liked Loriol no better than she liked Nicholas. The elder girl was invariably charming whenever they came into contact, but whatever she said she never failed to underline, in the most subtle and seemingly innocent way, the fact that she considered her employer's ward to be hopelessly juvenile.

Peta would have liked to believe that she took her cue from Nicholas, but in point of fact he took the greatest care to treat her with the most solemn and deferential courtesy. Since more often than not this was belied by that outrageous twinkle in his grey eyes she writhed inwardly, but there was nothing she could do about it. She couldn't brawl with him in public and she never saw him alone. Loriol made a pretty effective job of monopolising his attention. There was nothing in his attitude towards the Professor's secretary to suggest more than friendliness, but Peta thought it unlikely that his feelings were purely platonic. Loriol was lovely enough to make any man's heart beat a little faster—even a man as rude and arrogant and dictatorial as Nicholas Waring!

What he had said to her in the garden still rankled. "Do you think I'm too young for my age?" She surprised Richard Mayne with this question at the end of a long sitting, and he looked at her quizzically. That query didn't sound like Peta: her complete unselfconsciousness was, for him, part of her charm.

"I don't think so." He hesitated, struck by the unconscious appeal in her hazel eyes, and rather at a loss to know what to say, "Unsophisticated, yes, though that isn't quite the same thing."

"Isn't it?" Peta looked down, scuffing the toe of her sandal on the floor. "How d'you get it—sophistication, I mean?"

He gave an involuntary laugh. "Pray heaven you never find out, my child!"

"There!" Peta made a despairing gesture with her small sunburnt hands. "That's just what I mean! Even you call me a child!"

She could not quite keep the hurt note out of her voice and the man's eyes grew watchful. There was something behind this.

He said gently, "Don't scorn your youth, Peta. It's a precious gift: enjoy it while you can." Yet, even as he spoke, he felt a stab of misgiving. Peta *was* such a child. She had no weapon against the worldly armour of people who had long since left their innocence behind them.

He watched her as for the first time she wandered over to his easel and stood staring down at the canvas. It was already to her inexperienced eyes well on the way to being finished, and she was startled by the likeness he had caught. Yet was it so like? There was a vivid, glowing quality about that painted face that she was quite sure she did not possess, and to look at it made her feel suddenly shy.

"You have an enchanting face. . . ." Unbidden, Nicholas' words came into her mind and she bit her lip.

She turned away quickly, knocking over a small table as she did so.

"Well, do you like it?" Amused and touched both by her evident embarrassment and her clumsiness, Richard Mayne asked the question teasingly.

"You're a very good artist." Peta answered him guardedly. Then she added curiously, "Why did you want to paint me, Mr. Mayne? You could have found lots of girls far prettier."

He laughed. "Perhaps. Shall we say that I liked your freedom from any form of affectation? There are other reasons, but I don't propose to tell you them."

"Oh!" Peta looked at him, colouring hotly. "I wasn't fishing, you know."

"I do know, my dear." He regarded her thoughtfully. "How's the young Viking these days?"

Peta chuckled, relieved at the change of subject. "Poor Mike! Still under a cloud, I'm afraid. He's had to buy new canvas for *Romany* and it's left him stony broke. Sailing can be an expensive hobby, though of course it's well worth it."

Nothing wrong there, the man thought. Aloud he said, "And your guardian? Book going well?"

"I think so. Loriol—his secretary—is marvellously efficient and of course Dr. Waring is a great help."

Peta was careful to sound bright and enthusiastic. Much as she liked Richard Mayne, there were many things she could not bring herself to discuss with him. With the Mandevilles, however, she was far less inhibited, answering Holly's eager questions with a little more frankness than was perhaps wise.

"The secretary is jolly pretty, isn't she? Dickon saw her in the post office, buying some stamps, and he said she looked just like a film star," Holly said, her dark eyes sparkling.

"She is *very* pretty," Peta agreed. She looked at Mike and laughed. "I think even you might find her attractive, Mike, mini-skirt and false eyelashes notwithstanding!"

Mike, immersed in the *Yachting World,* merely grunted. He had already heard from several sources that the newcomer to Greylings was a stunner, but he wasn't particularly interested.

"And Dr. Waring? What about him?" Holly pressed. "Is he nice?"

"Ghastly!" Peta said grimly. "Conceited, arrogant, dictatorial—you name it, he is it!"

"Stars!" Holly looked at her with sympathy. "I suppose he can't help it. Old men do get cantankerous sometimes."

Peta's conscience pricked her. "He isn't old, not very. He's not much more than thirty, I'd say, if that. When he smiles he looks quite young."

"Is he stuffy?" Holly asked interestedly. "Does he like riding or sailing?"

"I don't know about riding. He can't sail: he says he's not interested. Personally I think he's afraid of getting his feet wet," Peta said acidly.

Mike threw down his magazine. "Oh, Lord, one of those!" he said, groaning, and again Peta's conscience troubled her. She had deliberately given them a false impression and she did not know why. She loathed Nicholas Waring, but she was fairly sure that there wasn't a cowardly or effeminate bone in his body. He looked as though he would be perfectly at home in any situation, however uncomfortable or dangerous, but she couldn't bring herself to say anything about him that might even remotely smack of commendation.

She had told Mike about their first meeting and been amused by his reaction.

"Wish I'd been there! I'd have knocked the silly chump's block off, speaking to you like that!" he'd said indignantly. Peta had laughed, cheered and comforted by his unhesitating partisanship, but she had wondered fleetingly whether Mike would have been able to do anything of the sort. Young Viking or not, he might have found Nicholas Waring more than his match.

Rather to Peta's surprise, Nicholas and Loriol announced their intention of accompanying herself and Ann to church on Sunday. Professor Devlin was the only one who elected to stay at home: years ago he had fallen out with the Rector and he still bore a grudge.

Annoyed with herself for her motives, Peta dressed herself with particular care, wishing that she had something a little smarter than the navy-blue linen suit which had served as her summer church-going outfit for the last two years. Not, she thought a little ruefully when she went downstairs to find Ann, Nicholas and Loriol already waiting in the hall, that anyone would notice what she had or hadn't got on: not with Loriol around. She looked even more attractive than usual this morning, with her face framed by an enchantingly pretty hat and wearing a beautifully tailored white suit which made Peta's outfit look shabbier than ever.

She felt Nicholas' eyes on her and went hot, even though his expression gave nothing away. At least he couldn't say she was wearing the wrong lipstick! Since that night she had thrown all her make-up away, and she was firmly resolved not to wear any again until she had the benefit of some expert advice. She wasn't going to risk making herself a figure of fun for a second time!

"Well, are we all ready?" Loriol asked gaily, and tucked her white gloved hand into Nicholas' arm as she spoke. She never lost an opportunity to stake her claim, Peta thought, and was surprised when a few moments later Nicholas made it clear that he expected Ann and not Loriol to occupy the front seat in his car. Glancing quickly at Loriol she saw a quiver of annoyance pass over her lovely face, but it had gone in an instant.

When they reached the little village church it was nearly full, the usual congregation having been swelled by the addition of a number of holidaymakers. It was quite easy to pick them out among the more conventionally attired villagers, but luckily the Rector was a tolerant man who considered that the fact that they had troubled to come to the service was far more important than what they wore.

As they walked up the narrow aisle to the Greylings pew Peta noticed Mrs. Mandeville, Mike, Holly and Dickon in their usual pew halfway up the right-hand side. She tried to catch Mike's eye, but to her amusement he was looking at Loriol, a startled expression on his face. Everyone else was looking at Loriol, too: she certainly knew how to attract attention, Peta thought ruefully, and then forgot all about her in her anxiety to manoeuvre things so she did not have to sit next to Nicholas Waring. To her surprise and annoyance her tactics failed miserably and she ended up with Ann on one side and Nicholas on the other. Worse, there were not enough hymn-books to go round and since Ann never used one—her eyesight was too poor to enable her to read small print and she knew most of the words by heart, anyway—she found herself forced to share with Nicholas. Why didn't he give her his book and share with Loriol? she thought indignantly, and wished that she were not so vitally aware of his nearness.

The rough tweed of his jacket pricked her cheek and she caught the faint and oddly pleasant aroma of the tobacco he always used. The fingers holding the hymn-book were hard and brown and strong. She did not realise how gingerly she was holding the other side until at the end of the second verse he bent down and said in her ear, "It won't bite, you know!"

Her face flamed and she glared. His eyes met hers, full of that hateful mocking laughter, and then she looked away and concentrated fiercely on the printed page in front of her. It was one of her favourite hymns: she wasn't going to let him spoil it for her! Luckily he had a very pleasant baritone voice and did not sing out of tune or off-key. That would have been the last straw!

When the service was over and they filed out into the sunshine the Rector greeted them at the church door. He smiled at Peta and Loriol and then shook hands with Nicholas, calling him by his name, before drawing Ann aside to congratulate her on her arrangement of the altar flowers. The church members took it in turns to supply these and Ann always outshone everyone else.

Loriol raised her brows enquiringly and Nicholas laughed.

"We met earlier in the week. I've had a good look

round the church: it's delightful, isn't it? Of course, Norfolk is famed for its beautiful churches."

Out of the corner of her eye Peta saw the Mandevilles approaching. She drew a deep breath, preparing to make the inevitable introductions, but found that no effort on her part was necessary.

"Good morning!" Margaret held out her hand to Nicholas with a charming smile. "I'm Margaret Mandeville and you, I am sure, are Dr. Waring. I've heard a lot about you from Peta, who is almost one of our family." She looked at Loriol and her tone became gaily confidential.

"Miss Kent, may I tell you something? Ever since you walked into church I've been admiring your enchanting hat and wondering where on earth you got it! Isn't that a frightful admission? I'm afraid I must be a very worldly woman!—worse, a frankly covetous one!"

Loriol laughed. "How nice of you to tell me so! I'm glad you like it: I got it from a funny little milliner in New York who makes the most marvellous hats and then sells them at fantastically low prices! I've told her that she could make a fortune if she really tried."

As she watched the little scene Peta was struck by the amazing similarity between the two women, not in features but in type. In some way, baffling description, they looked as if they belonged to the same world: even the vast discrepancy in their ages did not alter that fact.

"Why, they speak the same language," was the thought that flashed into Peta's mind, and then, "Goodness, anyone would think to hear them talk that a hat was *important*!"

She glanced at Mike, her eyes dancing, but no half-hidden smile answered her. He wasn't even looking in her direction.

Holly's round, dimpled face was full of suppressed excitement. She caught hold of Peta's arm and drew her aside.

"Peta, you *are* awful!" she whispered. "Why did you say all those horrid things about Dr. Waring? He looks an absolute *dish*! Not a bit like an archaeologist!"

"Shush!" Peta whispered back, her face burning, and hoped that nobody had heard.

"You must both come to supper one night," Margaret was saying gaily to Loriol. Her glance fell on Peta. "And Peta too, of course. What about tomorrow?"

"We'd love that, wouldn't we, Nicholas?" Loriol said with a smile. "It would make a very pleasant change. We've both been working full stretch ever since we came here."

So far Mike had said nothing at all, and Peta found his silence oddly disquieting. For once his easy self-assurance seemed to have deserted him: he seemed almost shy.

"What a good-looking face that Mandeville boy has," Loriol remarked carelessly on the way home. Then, as Peta instinctively stiffened, "Oh, of course he's a particular friend of yours, isn't he?" The green eyes were amused. "Your sailing companion, I presume?"

"Yes," Peta said tersely, and wondered why at that moment she should feel a prickle of apprehension. There wasn't any reason for it.

Or was there? At Cedar Lodge the following evening she felt an odd restriction of her throat as she saw Mike, that unfamiliar diffidence no longer apparent, laughing and talking with Loriol as if he had known her for years. It was obvious, indeed, that she and Nicholas had made a very favourable impression on the whole Mandeville family, but underneath the surface gaiety Peta sensed undercurrents which bewildered and even frightened her a little. For her the meal was not the comfortable occasion that it usually was: once again she had that unpleasant conviction that she was the odd one out, though she did her best to persuade herself that she was being ridiculous.

The meal was excellent; planned with care, beautifully cooked and attractively served. Peta, finding herself without gravy just as everyone else was about to begin their main course, asked Mike to pass it, but he did not seem to hear her. He was laughing at something Loriol had said, his vivid blue eyes glowing, and

Mrs. Mandeville was laughing too, her expression amused, almost indulgent, as she looked from one bright head to the other. If Mike looked like a Viking of elder days, Peta thought, then Loriol might equally well have been one of the bright-eyed, golden-haired daughters of the Northland. She bore far more resemblance to Mike, in colouring, than did his own sister.

She glanced quickly at Holly. She and Dickon were plying Nicholas with eager questions, to which, to do him justice, he was replying with patient good-humour. Holly, at any rate, was making no secret of the fact that she considered him 'a dish'. She was gazing at him with a rapt expression on her face, and in spite of herself Peta's lip curved into a reluctant smile. Holly had always got a crush on somebody or other: usually a pop star! She herself would have said that Nicholas was a most unlikely subject, but evidently Holly found something in him to admire. His looks, probably—he *was* good-looking, with those strongly marked cheekbones and jaw, well-cut lips and squarish chin with the faintest suggestion of a cleft. Unbidden, the thought came into her mind that there was a strength and purpose in his face which Mike's lacked and, dismayed, she crushed it. Mike was so much younger: it was unfair to compare them.

"Mike, will you pass Peta the gravy, please?" Nicholas, who evidently missed nothing, succeeded in making himself heard where Peta had failed and she flushed, biting her lip. She would rather have gone without the gravy than have Nicholas draw attention to any deficiencies on Mike's part.

Startled, Mike looked up. His eyes met Peta's for the first time that evening and he gave her a slightly shamefaced grin.

"Sorry, old thing! I didn't notice you hadn't had it. Why didn't you sing out?" He passed her the gravy and for a moment there was an odd little silence. Then Margaret Mandeville, leaning forward, asked brightly, "And what do you think of Norfolk, Dr. Waring? This is your first visit to East Anglia, isn't it?"

Nicholas's hesitation was only slight. "I haven't seen a

great deal yet. The scenery interests me, but I'm not altogether sure that I find it appealing. Its flatness is a bit monotonous: I prefer something a little more rugged."

"In other words, he's pining for his beloved mountains," Loriol said, smiling. She looked at Margaret. "Nicholas was born in the Lake District and his hobby is climbing. He's an expert mountaineer."

Dickon's eyes widened. "Are you really, Dr. Waring? I say, that's jolly interesting!"

It was evident that his opinion of Nicholas had immediately soared, but it was Holly who let her surprise betray her into a colossal breach of tact.

"You climb mountains? Oh, Peta, did you hear that? And you said you thought he'd be afraid to get his feet wet!" she exclaimed reproachfully.

Everyone heard her. Peta, who had since regretted that unfortunate observation, wished the floor would open up and swallow her. Loriol raised delicately arched brows, Dickon choked on a piece of chicken and Mike glared at his young sister in a way which made her flush scarlet to the roots of her hair. Even Margaret seemed at a loss to know how to retrieve the situation until Nicholas, seemingly unperturbed, said pleasantly, "I'm afraid Peta has a very low opinion of anyone who doesn't share her enthusiasm for sailing. You do, I believe, Mike?"

Mike grinned, thankfully seizing the opportunity to divert the conversation into safer channels.

"Rather. I'm very keen."

"And that," said his mother with mock despair, "is the understatement of the year!" She looked enquiringly at Loriol. "Do you sail, Miss Kent?"

Loriol shook her head regretfully. "I'm afraid not. I've never had the chance to learn, but of course I'd love to."

"Then you must get Mike to take you out in his dinghy one evening. I'm sure he'd be only too glad to give you a lesson or two, wouldn't you Mike?" Margaret said sweetly.

Peta shot her an incredulous glance. It seemed to be

an evening for blunders: Mike's aversion to teaching people how to sail was well known to all his family. There was, however, not the slightest hint of reluctance or embarrassment in his manner as he said eagerly, "Yes, of course I will. Let me know when you're free and we'll fix something up."

"How very nice of you. I'll certainly look forward to that," Loriol told him. Just for a moment her eyes met Peta's and in their green depths was amusement and—yes, an unmistakable gleam of triumph.

Peta bent her head, crumbling her roll between suddenly nerveless fingers. Then, determined not to reveal her dismay, she looked up, her expression unconsciously defiant. She had intended to make a light-hearted observation, but the words died on her lips. She saw Nicholas staring at Loriol, frowning slightly, and with a quick flash of intuition realised that he did not care for the idea of Loriol receiving lessons from Mike. It was natural enough: she had very little free time at the moment and obviously he did not want anyone else to monopolise it.

Peta tried to tell herself that she, at any rate, had no proprietorial rights where Mike was concerned. And at least he made it clear, when later they were alone together for a few minutes, that he expected her to help him with Loriol's tuition.

"I couldn't very well refuse to take her out in *Romany*," he said, sounding, Peta thought, a little too much on the defensive. "Mum put me in rather a spot, asking me straight out like that in front of her." He hesitated, then added with a kind of awkward, embarrassed honesty, "But actually I don't mind all that much. She's a—well, she's a frightfully nice girl, isn't she? Not a bit like I expected." There was a hint of accusation in his voice.

Peta felt an odd pang. She did not, at that moment, recognise it as jealousy, but it was only with an effort that she managed to answer calmly.

"I'm glad you like her."

"Well, I do. Waring seems quite a nice chap, too. You certainly jumped to the wrong conclusions about him, you old muggins! A bloke who's not afraid to climb a ruddy great mountain can't be much of a cissy!" •

Peta bit her lip. She had an uneasy feeling that although Nicholas had showed no annoyance when Holly had repeated what she had said about him, she had by no means heard the last of the incident. Somehow she did not think he was the sort of person one could insult with impunity—and yet what could he do about it if she took care to keep out of his way? Nothing, she told herself firmly, and even managed to believe it until two days later she emerged from the boathouse after lunch to find Nicholas standing on the river bank, deep in conversation with Stephen Norwell.

Startled, she would have instantly retreated, but Stephen turned his head and saw her.

"Oh, Peta! There you are!" He came towards her, and Nicholas followed. "A new pupil for you—well, new in a manner of speaking, that is!"

Unaware of the constrained relationship between the two, he spoke cheerfully, and did not notice Peta's expression.

"Pupil?" she echoed blankly. She looked from one man to the other. Nicholas was more informally dressed than she had ever seen him, in an open-necked, short-sleeved shirt and grey flannels, and with a white sweater flung casually over one shoulder. Oh, surely Stephen didn't mean . . . *couldn't* mean. . . .

"I've heard so much about the delights of sailing from you and Mike that I decided it was high time that I experienced them for myself." Nicholas spoke easily and only Peta realised the significance of that dancing light in his grey eyes. "You'll take me on, won't you, Peta? I promise I'll do exactly what I'm told—provided that you promise, in your return, not to drown me!"

"Not much fear of that!" Stephen said, laughing. "Peta is an excellent instructress. I can safely leave you in her hands, Waring." He clapped Peta on the shoulder. "Wind's southerly and freshening. I'd take the *Swallow* if I were you."

He raised his hand in a careless salute and strode off in the direction of the boathouse. Peta turned to Nicholas, her small chin very much in evidence.

"I suppose this is your idea of a joke?"

Nicholas laughed and thrust his hands deep into his pockets. She suspected that he was hugely enjoying himself.

"Does a man usually expose himself to mortal danger just for a joke?"

"Mortal danger?" She echoed his words without thinking and a moment later could have kicked herself.

"Why, of getting my feet wet, of course!" Nicholas said blandly.

She had asked for that. Not trusting herself to answer, she led the way over to the *Swallow*, climbed in and untied it. The only course open to her, she decided grimly, was to try to treat Nicholas exactly as if he were an ordinary pupil. Why he had come she hadn't the slightest idea, unless his intention was to cause her embarrassment. If so, he had already succeeded. Perhaps because he so obviously thought of her as a gauche teenager, she found herself behaving like one in his presence.

She wondered fleetingly if Loriol knew where he was, and then there was no opportunity to wonder about anything else. From the moment they moved out into the river she discovered how right Stephen had been about the freshening wind. It seemed to be getting stronger every minute and it kept veering, so that it was all that she could do to keep the small dinghy steady on its course. The wind, pressing on the sail, seemed to be trying to lift the rudder out of the water and that made steering difficult.

Peta, hanging on to the mainsheet with one hand and gripping the tiller as hard as she could with the other, reefed as soon as she could, doing her best to keep the dinghy from yawing about. It was not ideal weather in which to teach anyone to sail, but after a time she had grudgingly to admit to herself that Nicholas was behaving surprisingly well. He spoke only when it was necessary—some people kept up a barrage of stupid questions!—he listened carefully to her instructions and obeyed them promptly, and, wonder of wonders, he actually appeared to be enjoying himself. Peta, always patient, sympathetic and encouraging with her pupils, almost forgot that this was the man she disliked so intensely and that his reasons for being here were definitely suspect. Like her, he seemed caught up in the exhilaration of the moment: the sun was bright, the water sparkled, and the gulls were swift against the summer sky. Even though the wind was so rough and squally it was better than no wind at all, though of course it made sailing a tricky business.

She wondered, involuntarily, whether Mike would risk taking Loriol out in this sort of weather. Probably not—conditions like these would put a lot of beginners right off. But not Nicholas. She stole a surreptitious glance at his silent figure. Although he had claimed to have no affinity with water, he looked perfectly relaxed and at ease. He must have felt her gaze, for he turned his head and smiled, his eyes crinkling at the corners. She smiled back with something approaching her normal friendliness. Perhaps he wasn't so bad after all.

There weren't many other boats out. In fact, they seemed to have this particular stretch of the river almost to themselves, or so she thought until on their way back they were almost capsized by a high-powered motor boat. Blaring out 'pop' music and crowded with young people, it roared round a bend and rushed full speed towards them. There was nothing Peta could do except giving an indignant shout: last-minute evasive action by the grinning skipper averted a nasty collision, but both Nicholas and Peta were drenched with spray and the dinghy rocked perilously in the heavy wash.

"Idiots! That's how accidents happen!" Peta, wrenching hard on the tiller, glared after the retreating boat. "I don't suppose they ever take the trouble to remember that the river's got a right side and a wrong side!"

"Just like the road, in fact. But then not everyone

remembers the Highway Code, do they?" Nicholas murmured.

His voice was mild, but his lips twitched. Peta saw the mocking glint in his eyes and knew exactly what thought was passing through his mind. All her old antagonism came flooding back in full force and as he let go his hold to pick up something that had clattered on to the deck she yielded to a blind impulse. Deliberately, she brought the dinghy round to put the wind abeam and tilt her. Immediately the craft heeled farther over to port and the deck slope sharpened, so that Nicholas, losing his balance, shot down and crashed across the wet and slippery floorboards.

For Peta it was an appalling moment. She knew perfectly well that she had lost her temper and tilted the dinghy on purpose, regardless of the fact that Nicholas was her pupil and that in a sense she was responsible for his safety. However much he had provoked her there was no excuse for what she had done. In trying to humiliate him she had succeeded only in humiliating herself.

Nicholas picked himself up and she saw with horror that there was a slight gash in the middle of his forehead. It was bleeding a little.

"Are you all right?" Her voice shook. She desperately wanted to say she was sorry, but she could not find the words.

"Yes, thanks." He began to staunch the blood with a clean white handkerchief, then, seeing her expression, added quickly, "Don't worry. It wasn't much of a bump. My fault—I should have been hanging on."

He sounded cheerfully matter-of-fact, but Peta wondered, with a feeling of sick misery, if he suspected that her manoeuvre had been deliberate. If he did then he deserved full marks for self-control. He had a right to be furious—as Stephen Norwell would be if he ever had an inkling about what had happened. He'd probably sack her on the spot and he'd be right, she told herself bitterly. She didn't deserve a position of trust.

Stephen was, in fact, waiting for them at the landing

stage when they got back. He gave an exclamation of concern as Nicholas stepped out of the dinghy.

"Good lord! What's happened to you?"

Peta opened her mouth, but Nicholas forestalled her.

"I slipped. Haven't found my sea legs yet," he said calmly. "Nothing to worry about—it's only a scratch." He looked down at Peta, who was fastening the painter. "Thanks for the lesson, Peta. I enjoyed it."

His smile was friendly, but his expression was enigmatic. Peta, concentrating fiercely on the knot she was tying, mumbled something inaudible, and when she next looked up his tall figure had gone.

CHAPTER FIVE

PETA left the river that evening feeling so disgusted and disappointed with herself that she telephoned Ann and said she would not be home for dinner. She simply could not face the thought of sitting opposite Nicholas at dinner feeling as she did, guilty and ashamed.

Instead, she decided to go and spend an hour or two with Richard Mayne. She knew that he would welcome her—he always seemed pleased to see her, and probably she would cook a light meal for them both. She'd done that once or twice before, not that she could cook anything elaborate, but her omelettes weren't too bad. Even Mike approved of those.

Her face shadowed at the thought of Mike. Ordinarily, whenever she was in any kind of trouble she turned instinctively to Mike . . . but not this time. It wasn't just that he would slate her for what she had done. He and she had always spoken their minds to each other. It was . . . well, it was just that things seemed different now, that was all. She didn't attempt to analyse why they were different, perhaps because she was afraid that the answer would be too disturbing.

Driving over to Richard Mayne's cottage, she decided that she would tell the artist the whole story. If he advised her to confess and apologise to Nicholas the next time she saw him she would do it, even though it would be the hardest thing she had ever done in her life. He would probably retaliate with some scathing remark about her immaturity, she thought, and sighed. She supposed that on the river this afternoon she *had* behaved like a silly, irresponsible child, but just at the moment she felt very old indeed.

The tiny, rather dilapidated little cottage that Richard had rented for the summer looked deserted when she got there, but she knew it was unlikely that he would be out. He had no car and too much walking seemed to tire him. He'd hinted once that he was supposed to rest far more than he was doing: he looked awfully grey sometimes. She had a vague idea that there was something wrong with his heart, but the subject was never mentioned between them.

She tapped lightly on the door, which was slightly ajar, and waited for Richard to call 'Come in'. There was, however, complete silence, and after two or three minutes she tapped again. Still no answer. He couldn't be out . . . he'd have closed the door.

Puzzled, she walked round to the window and peeped inside. At what she saw she gave a gasp of horror. Richard Mayne was slumped in an armchair, and it was obvious from the stillness of his huddled figure and his queer colour that he was either unconscious . . . or dead.

Not dead. Kneeling beside him a few seconds later Peta realised with a feeling of wild relief that his heart was still beating, though it was barely perceptible. She noticed that his thin, blue-veined hand was clenched round a small bottle of tablets that he always kept by him: evidently he had been trying to take one when he had collapsed.

Trying frantically to remember the smattering of First Aid she had picked up at school, she loosened the unconscious man's collar and tie and then rose to her feet, looking down at him with frightened eyes. If only he did not look such a deathly colour! For a moment she gave way to a feeling of utter helplessness, then she pulled herself together. Whatever was wrong with him he was obviously seriously ill and medical attention was urgently required. There was nothing more she could do for him: the doctor must be called at once. She thought desperately. There was no telephone in the cottage or in those nearby: the nearest was the kiosk in the village, but Greylings was not much further away and in the long run it would probably be quicker to phone from there.

At Greylings she left her car with the engine still running and flew into the hall. There was nobody else about as she lifted the receiver with shaking fingers and dialled the doctor's number. Luckily it was he himself who answered: she had been dreading to be told that he was out.

Dr. Myers did not waste a second after hearing her breathless story. She did not know it, but Richard Mayne had consulted him at his surgery the previous week and he had the artist's case history at his fingertips.

"I'll come at once, but I'm bound to be a few minutes. Will you go back to the patient, my dear, and stay with him until I arrive? If he's conscious keep him quiet: cover him over with something warm, but don't attempt to move him."

Peta replaced the receiver and leant against the wall for a moment for support. "If he's conscious. . . ." Richard Mayne's grey face swam before her eyes. His heart-beat had been so faint. Suppose . . . suppose when she got back to the cottage. . . .

"Peta." Nicholas stood beside her and stupidly, inexplicably, the kindness of his voice almost made her break down. "I was in the library: I couldn't help hearing what you were saying just now. Is there anything I can do to help?"

Peta forgot everything except the one fact that here was someone who was strong and solid and reassuring. She raised her anxious eyes to his.

"It—it's a great friend of mine. He's very ill: I found him unconscious a few minutes ago. The doctor is coming as soon as he can, I'm going back and stay with him until he arrives."

Afterwards she remembered that Nicholas did not even hesitate.

"Would you like me to come with you?"

"Oh!" She gave an incredulous gasp. *"Would* you? But why should you—I mean. . . ."

"Give me credit for a little decency! Of course I'll come if you want me to. I suppose that's your car outside with the engine running? Switch it off: we'll go in mine," Nicholas said crisply.

Peta did not argue. It did not even occur to her to do so: Nicholas was already so much in command of the situation. In what seemed to her to be an incredibly short time she was back at the cottage and Nicholas was bending over the artist's huddled figure.

Watching in silent suspense, she heaved a sigh of profound relief as Richard Mayne's eyes opened and he murmured something in a feeble voice. Nicholas answered him gently, then turned to Peta.

"He's conscious but very muzzy: doesn't seem to know where he is or even who you are. Go and see if you can find a couple of rugs or blankets to put over him, Peta, his hands are like ice. Anything warm will do."

"Is he—do you think he's going to be all right?"

"Yes," Nicholas answered her briefly but with confidence. His face intent, he was holding Richard's thin wrist, listening to his pulse.

Peta, disappearing into the tiny cubicle which served as the artist's bedroom, could only be thankful for his calm competence. Unlike her guardian, he did not live in an ivory tower: she could not imagine how the Professor would have reacted to a situation like this.

There was only one thin blanket on Richard Mayne's narrow camp bed. She gave this to Nicholas and then returned to the bedroom to see if there were any more stored in a cupboard. A few moments later a car pulled up outside the cottage and she heard Dr. Myers' familiar gruff voice greeting his patient. He had completed a brief examination and was preparing an injection when, carrying a plaid rug that she had found under a pile of clean bed-linen, she returned to the studio.

"That's a nasty attack you've had this time, Mr. Mayne," the doctor was saying. "I told you last week that you'd have to take more care of yourself."

"I did," Richard Mayne protested weakly.

"Humph!" said Dr. Myers disbelievingly. "Well, you'll be well enough cared for now: I'm sending you to hospital for a day or two. I took the precaution of phoning for an ambulance before I left home."

"Hospital? Why can't I stay here?" Richard Mayne demanded, and there was a sudden and remarkable addition of strength to his voice.

Dr. Myers gave him a grim smile. "Because in your

present state of health hospital is the best place for you. Don't you agree, my dear?" He looked towards Peta as he spoke.

Richard's sunken eyes followed the direction of his gaze and his pallid lips curved into a little smile.

"I hear that you found me. Lucky for me you dropped in this evening, but I'm sorry if I gave you a shock, child."

Peta came forward and clasped the thin cold hand that was held out to her. It felt as dry and brittle as an autumn leaf.

"It doesn't matter since you're going to be all right. I'll come and see you in hospital, Mr. Mayne."

"That's a promise, mind you," the artist said. His voice sounded a little weaker and after a moment he closed his eyes. At a nod from the doctor Peta gently withdrew her fingers and went to join Nicholas, who was standing by the window.

He regarded her thoughtfully, an odd expression on his brown face.

"Mayne? That's his name?"

"Yes. He's an artist, as you've probably guessed from all the paraphernalia lying around."

"Not . . . Richard Mayne, by any chance?" There was an almost incredulous note in Nicholas's voice and Peta looked at him, startled.

"Yes. Why? What do you know about him?"

Before he could answer the ambulance arrived. Peta watched while the attendants, kindly and efficient, carried Richard Mayne out on a stretcher, then shook her head as the doctor asked her if she knew of anyone who might like to be notified of the fact that he was in hospital.

"No." She hesitated. "I—I don't think he has any relatives. He's never mentioned anyone." She could have added, but didn't, that it was his loneliness which had first aroused her compassion.

Nicholas made as if to speak, then obviously thought better of it. He waited until Dr. Myers had gone, then turned to Peta with raised brows.

"Well, what now?" he asked quietly.

Peta brushed her hand across her eyes. "I—I don't know. I suppose we'd better lock up." She bent to pick up a book which was lying on the floor and a sudden thought struck her.

"Nicholas, he hasn't got any of his things! Pyjamas . . . dressing-gown . . . toothbrush . . . shaving gear . . . oh, I ought to have thought of all that before!"

"You needn't worry. The hospital will provide him with anything he needs," Nicholas told her.

"Yes, but. . . ." Peta bit her lip, her face troubled. It was one small thing she could have done for Richard, and she had failed to do it.

A faint smile touched Nicholas's lips. "But you think he'd like to have his own things? Perhaps you're right, Peta. Pack a small suitcase and we'll take it to the hospital now."

Peta flushed. She said quickly, "There's no need . . . I mean, I could take it myself."

"You could, but I don't think you should." Nicholas sounded brusque. "You look all in, and small wonder."

Peta opened her mouth to contradict him, then closed it again. It was true. She didn't really feel up to driving any distance: she felt deathly tired, almost drained, and a bit cold and sick.

She packed a small attaché case and joined Nicholas in his car. Throughout the journey to the hospital he drove fast and skilfully and at first in complete silence. Peta leaned back in her seat and tried not to think. The speed of the car soothed her and the burden of her anxiety for Richard pressed less heavily. She felt a swift rush of gratitude towards Nicholas. If only he had always been as kind and understanding as he had been tonight!

She stole a surreptitious look at his profile.

A lock of black hair had fallen across his forehead and he put up his hand to brush it away. As he did so he touched the livid bruise which was his memento of his afternoon on the river and Peta saw him wince slightly. Memories of the day's events came crowding back into her mind and she sat suddenly tense and rigid.

As if he felt the change in her attitude Nicholas

spoke for the first time since they left the cottage.

"Have you known Richard Mayne long?"

"Only a week or two. He's rented the cottage for the whole summer, I think." She recalled Nicholas's surprise when he had discovered the artist's identity and repeated the question that at that time had gone unanswered.

"What do you know about Mr. Mayne, Nicholas?" She used his Christian name without thinking.

"Only that he's one of the best known portrait painters in Europe," Nicholas said drily. He turned his head and caught the look of stupefaction on her face. "You didn't know? But surely——"

He stopped short and Peta felt the colour rush into her face. What a little ignoramus he must think her! She *hadn't* realised that Richard was famous—but she *had* recognised his extraordinary talent! She said defensively, "It doesn't make any difference to me whether he's famous or not! I like people for what they are, not for what they've achieved!"

"How very right you are," Nicholas approved, and there might or might not have been a tremor of laughter in his voice. Peta looked at him with a certain amount of suspicion, but he was poker-faced. She would have liked to have pursued the subject of Richard Mayne further, but by now they had reached the outskirts of the town and Nicholas was obliged to give his full attention to the hazards of the heavy traffic. Only when he had pulled into the hospital car park did he speak again.

"You'll have to find out what ward he's in. Want me to come with you?"

Peta's chin went up. His moral support had sustained her so far, but she could quite well do without it.

"I can manage, thank you."

He glanced at his wristwatch. "It's visiting time, judging by that board over there. They may let you see him, but don't count on it. Anyway, you needn't hurry—I'll phone Greylings while you're gone and explain what's happened. It's suddenly occurred to me

77

that we ought to account to your Aunt Ann for our absence."

He means Loriol, Peta thought. He wants Loriol to know where he is. Aloud she said, "Ann wasn't expecting me home for dinner, but probably everyone is wondering what has happened to you. There's a phone box over there: did you see it?"

"Yes, I did. After I've phoned I'll wait for you in the car."

He escorted her as far as the phone box, then she went on alone to Reception. She felt curiously bereft without the comfort of his presence. Comfort . . . that was an odd word to use in connection with Nicholas, she thought wryly, but nevertheless at the moment it was the right one.

She found out from Reception that Richard was in a private ward in the east wing and made her way there. She handed the suitcase to a friendly, bright-faced Sister who told her that Richard was resting, probably by now asleep.

"You can peep at him through the window if you like, but don't disturb him," she was told. Then, curiously, "Are you his daughter?"

Peta shook her head. "No. Just a friend."

She tiptoed along the corridor and peeped through the window into Richard's small white cubicle. As the Sister had conjectured, he was sleeping, and already looking, Peta noted with a rush of relief, considerably better. She was glad he was in a private ward, though if Nicholas hadn't told her what he had she might have worried about his ability to pay for it! 'One of the best known portrait painters in Europe. . . .' She had been quite wrong, then, when she had surmised that perhaps he had been embittered by lack of success, but she hadn't been wrong about his loneliness. Why, she wondered, had a man like Richard Mayne elected to turn his back on the world he knew and retreat to an obscure little Norfolk village? Oh, he was ill, anyone could see that, but surely that made his decision even more puzzling. Wasn't there anyone who cared about him, not just as a famous artist but as a man?

Her face was sober as she went back to the car, where Nicholas was waiting for her, seemingly absorbed in thought. He was smoking one of his favourite Turkish cigarettes, but he stubbed it out and threw it away when he saw her approaching.

"Everything all right?" He opened the door for her to get in and switched on the engine.

"Yes, thank you. I didn't see Mr. Mayne to talk to, he was asleep, but Sister said that was the best thing for him and that he'd probably be a lot better in a day or two. Oh, and she said he'd be awfully glad to have his own things."

"Good." Nicholas let in the clutch and swung the car out of the hospital car park. He seemed disinclined to talk and Peta, tired and preoccupied as she was, took some little time to realise that they were heading for the town centre.

"We're going the wrong way!" she said sharply. "You should have turned right back there, at the traffic lights."

Nicholas shook his head. "I'm not taking you home just yet," he said calmly. "I think that first and foremost we both need something to eat."

"No!" Already racked by tension, Peta felt her heart plunge in ridiculous panic. "No, Nicholas, we can't! Ann will be expecting us! You did telephone her, didn't you?"

"I did, and she won't be. Expecting us, I mean. I told her I was taking you out to a meal and she appeared to think it was an extremely good idea." Nicholas spoke as calmly as before.

"But I'm not hungry!"

Nicholas said nothing further until he had brought the car to a halt outside a big, neon-lighted hotel. Then he turned his head to look down at her with a grim little smile.

"That's utter nonsense, my dear, and well you know it. I realise that you probably dislike me so much that you feel you can't wait to rid yourself of my company, but don't you think that we could agree to forget our differences for another half hour or so? Personally I'm

79

famished and I'm quite certain, whatever your protestations to the contrary, that you must be too." He paused and then added, with that old mocking gleam back in his eyes, "Remember you can't fight on an empty stomach!"

He was right about one thing. She *was* starving, though up to now she had not realised it. But he was wrong about the other thing he had said. It wasn't because she disliked him that she was reluctant to fall in with his suggestion. It was because of her guilty conscience, which had been pricking her at intervals ever since they left the cottage.

Scarlet-cheeked, she said wretchedly, "You just don't understand. I—you've been so terribly kind tonight and I feel such a *worm*!"

She saw the astonishment on his face and heard him laugh, but she took a deep breath and went on doggedly and not very coherently.

"I—this afternoon on the river, it was all my fault that you fell and hit your head. I *meant* you to. At least, I didn't mean you to hurt yourself and I'm awfully sorry that you did, but I wanted you to lose your balance and feel silly. I—I tilted the dinghy on purpose. It was an awful thing to do and I deserve to lose my job, but—but you were making fun of me and I couldn't bear it." She stopped, then added miserably, "I would have told you the truth and said I was sorry even if you hadn't been so nice to me tonight, but now that you have been it's worse than ever. You laughed when I said it, but it's true, I *do* feel a worm, an absolute *crawling* worm!"

There was a moment's silence, then Nicholas said very gently, "You didn't really have to tell me what happened this afternoon, Peta. I'd already guessed. But I didn't mind. I rather felt that I'd got what I deserved."

She shook her head. "You were my pupil. It was awful of me."

"Well, if you really feel so guilty about it I'll allow you to make reparation by being very, very nice to me while we're having dinner," Nicholas said, laughing.

His voice was amused, but his eyes were warm and

kindly. Why, he's *nice*, Peta thought incredulously. It was odd she hadn't realised it before. Or perhaps it wasn't so odd. The memory of their first meeting had rankled so much that after that every time he had smiled or teased her she had deliberately turned it into something unkind or hurtful.

The hotel he had chosen, apparently at random, boasted a beautifully appointed dining room where the tables were set back in alcoves, lit by soft wall lights that cast a rosy gleam over white damask and shining silver and centrepieces of delicate, fragrant flowers.

"Aren't they lovely? I'm glad they're not plastic," Peta said, touching one velvety bloom with a gentle forefinger.

"The real thing or nothing at all? I feel rather like that, too," Nicholas said, smiling. He held out the menu, which seemed to be of formidable proportions. "Would you like to choose?"

"Not if it's all in French," Peta said candidly. "I'm not very good at it. You choose for me. There isn't anything I don't like, except oysters, and I'd probably like those if I was blindfolded while I ate them!"

She looked appreciatively around her while Nicholas studied the menu. Disconcertingly she encountered her reflection in a big wall mirror, and at what she saw she gave a sudden gasp of dismay.

"Nicholas, you forget! My clothes! I—I'm not dressed for a place like this!" With horror she realised that she was still wearing the jeans and shirt which formed her working gear: the only woman in the room who had obviously taken no trouble with her appearance. All the others had sleek, shining hair and carefully made-up faces and they wore dresses which seemed to her to be the very latest in fashion.

"Why worry?" Nicholas asked. "You're still the prettiest girl here and would be if you wore sackcloth and ashes!"

It was charmingly said, but Peta, hot with embarrassment, wondered if secretly he was comparing her with Loriol. *She* would never appear in public looking anything but beautiful and well-groomed and soignée! No doubt she had been out to dinner with Nicholas on many occasions and he had been proud to be seen in her company! There would have been none of the furtive, amused stares which she fancied were now being directed at their table!

Self-consciousness was not a thing from which normally she suffered and at first it made her shy, but she soon found that when Nicholas exerted himself to be charming it was impossible for shyness to last. The dinner was excellent and they both did justice to it: courses came, delicious and appetising, and the empty plates vanished as if by magic. Nicholas ordered champagne—"Yes, aren't I extravagant? But it's the only way to cement a new-found friendship," he said, laughing—and they talked to each other with perfect ease and familiarity. It seemed to Peta that Nicholas avoided mentioning his work, but he talked entertainingly on a variety of other subjects. She, in turn, responded eagerly to his skilful questioning and told him about Norfolk and sailing and the many experiences she had shared with Mike on the Broads.

Nicholas listened intently, his head bent, watching the bubbles in his glass. Suddenly his eyes lifted and he gave her an unexpectedly searching look.

"Mike is a specially good friend of yours, I take it?"

"Why—yes, of course." Taken aback, Peta stared at him. "Why do you ask?"

"Only because he seems to have played a pretty prominent part in your life so far," Nicholas said lightly. "I don't think you've said 'I' once, it's been 'we' all the time. It sounds rather like Darby and Joan!"

There was a moment's silence. Peta wanted to laugh and make a rejoinder in the same light-hearted vein, but for some reason she found it impossible. Instead, to her intense annoyance and embarrassment she found herself blushing hotly, until her face and neck were covered by a crimson tide.

She saw Nicholas's lips quirk and knew quite well what he must be thinking. He made no further comment, however, but adroitly changed the subject. Peta felt uncomfortably that he had been left with the wrong impression and wished she could correct it, but that was easier said than done. She could hardly blurt out, à propos of nothing, that she and Mike were merely very good friends.

Nicholas was talking now about her guardian.

"It's a pity you and he don't try to get on to the same wavelength, Peta. He's got his points, you know, though I do admit he can be intensely irritating at times."

"It's no good. I'm a fearful disappointment to him," Peta said ruefully. She added incautiously, "He'd much rather have someone intelligent and accomplished like Loriol."

She saw his face go blank.

"Loriol is doing a very good job of work for him at the moment. Naturally he's grateful, but I don't suppose it goes further than that."

Peta did not argue. Instead she traced an intricate pattern on the tablecloth with her coffee spoon. Without looking up she asked with studied casualness, "How long do you think it will be before the book is finished?"

"Hard to say. They've made pretty good progress so far, but then they've both worked like Trojans."

"You've helped a lot, too," Peta reminded him.

"Yes, but I'm afraid my usefulness is coming to an end. I ought to be making a move, even though the Professor keeps urging me to stay."

This time Peta did look up. "And will you? Stay, I mean?"

She knew, from what he had already told her, that he had no home in England. His parents had both died several years ago and he appeared to have no other close ties.

For a moment he was silent, as though he was weighing the matter in his mind. Then he said slowly, "Yes. Yes, I think I will, for a little longer."

Of course, thought Peta, he wants to be with Loriol. Perhaps they would even get engaged when the book was finished. Somehow the idea chilled her, though she did not know why.

At any rate he ought to be getting back to Loriol now. She said childishly, "Don't you think we ought to be going? It must be awfully late."

He glanced at his watch. "Good heavens, yes! It's nearly ten o'clock. It's a wonder we weren't thrown out long ago!"

He paid the bill and they went out to the car. For most of the journey home both were silent, but it was, Peta felt, a companionable silence. There would be no more friction or bickering between her and Nicholas. She would never forget how much he had helped her tonight, though when they reached Greylings and stammeringly she tried to thank him he merely laughed and refused to listen.

"I've had a most delightful evening," he said, smiling. "It is I who should thank you, not the other way round!"

Ann came hurrying to meet them when she heard Peta's key in the lock.

"I'm just making coffee," she told them. "It's nearly ready. Go in the sitting room, both of you, and I'll bring it in. Loriol is there, she'll be glad of your company, I expect. I'm afraid it's been a very dull evening for her."

One look at Loriol's stony face was enough to proclaim the truth of Ann's words. She was sitting curled up in an armchair, flicking over the pages of a magazine, and when Nicholas and Peta came in she gave them a cold stare and a barely civil greeting.

"All alone?" Nicholas asked pleasantly. "Where's the Professor?"

"He went off to bed ages ago. Migraine," Loriol answered him shortly. "I've been sitting here all evening just twiddling my thumbs! I've never been so bored in all my life!" She paused, then added sulkily, "You told me you'd take me out somewhere the first free evening I had!"

Peta shot a dismayed look at Nicholas, but he seemed quite unperturbed by Loriol's bad temper.

"I'm sorry about that, but I'm afraid it couldn't be

84

helped. I expect Miss Devlin has told you the whole story? I telephoned her earlier this evening."

Loriol hunched an impatient shoulder. "She told me some rigmarole about some old artist who'd had a heart attack! I really can't imagine how you came to be involved!"

"I'm a Boy Scout at heart, didn't you know?" Nicholas mocked. He searched in his pocket for his cigarette case and took one out.

Loriol gave him a glittering glance. Peta, feeling distinctly uncomfortable, spoke awkwardly.

"I don't really think I want coffee, Nicholas. I'm awfully tired. Will you tell Aunt Ann I've gone to bed, please? And—and thank you again for tonight."

She turned and went out of the room. Nicholas wouldn't be able to make his peace with Loriol while she was there. Not, she thought wryly, that he was going to have an easy task in any circumstances. For some reason—which surely had little to do with the fact that for one evening she had been left to her own devices—Loriol was obviously very angry indeed.

CHAPTER SIX

PETA telephoned the hospital first thing next morning and was told that Richard Mayne had spent a restful night and that his condition had improved. Greatly relieved, she drove over to see him directly she had finished work for the day, and was rewarded by the way in which his tired face lit up the moment she walked into his room.

"Peta, my dear! How nice of you to come! I knew you would keep your promise, but I didn't dare hope that it would be so soon."

Peta crossed over to his bed with a light step. She was glad she had come: he looked so frail and so utterly alone.

"I've brought you these, from Ann's garden." She laid a bunch of fragrant, glowing roses beside him and silently, with his look, the artist paid tribute to their beauty.

"I've been talking to your nice Sister. She says you're very much better, although I gather you're far from being a model patient!"

"That shouldn't surprise you," Richard said ruefully. "After a lifetime of self-indulgence I don't take too kindly to hospital rules and regulations! But nevertheless here I am and here, it seems, I have to stay, for a few days at least. I've been told so many times that I'm in the best place that perhaps in time I shall almost come to believe it." He looked at her and sighed. "I only wish I had finished your portrait, child."

"Oh, but there'll be plenty of time for that," Peta said quickly. She hesitated and flushed a little. "I—I hope you don't mind, but—but I know who you are now. Nicholas—Dr. Waring, whom you met last night—says you're a famous portrait painter. I—I suppose I ought to have known, but I didn't."

A faint smile touched the pale lips. "Does it make any difference?"

She shook her head. "None. But," she added naïvely,

86

"I suppose I ought to consider it a great honour to have my portrait painted by you, oughtn't I?"

"I don't see why you should. Fortunately your mind doesn't work that way." Richard spoke with a certain amount of dryness and changed the subject skilfully. "Will you thank Dr. Waring for me when you next see him? He appears to have been most kind. I can't truthfully say that I remember much about last night, but I am indeed grateful to you both. Perhaps you'll bring him to see me when I'm home again?"

"Yes. I think you'd like each other," Peta said. She didn't really want to talk about Nicholas and she looked at him a little anxiously, a tentative question forming itself upon her lips.

"Is there anyone you'd like to visit you in hospital? I could always write a letter for you, or telephone."

She was unprepared for the bitterness which washed over the thin face.

"There's no one," he said harshly, and though she did not understand the tone of his voice, something about it chilled her to the bone. His expression was suddenly bleak, and his eyes looked very tired and sad.

Dismayed, she went on talking as brightly as she could, searching for something that might cheer him. Once or twice she did coax a smile from him, but it was a forced smile and when she left, at the end of an hour, it was with the conviction that he had some anxiety weighing heavily on his mind.

She stopped on the way home at Cedar Lodge. She had seen nothing at all of Mike during the last day or two and he had only telephoned once. That had merely been to confirm that she had sent in their entry for Horning Regatta, which was in three weeks' time. This was an event to which they were both looking forward. They had been very successful in previous years and Peta knew that Mike thought that they stood a good chance of winning their class for the third year running, If, in fact, they did it would be against stiff opposition and they would have every right to feel jubilant.

Just at this moment, saddened by her visit to Richard, Peta longed for Mike's cheery companionship, and her face fell when Mrs. Mandeville informed her that he was out.

"Will he be very long, do you think? Is it any good my waiting?" For once Peta, usually sensitive to atmosphere, failed to notice Margaret's lack of cordiality.

"I really don't know, Peta." The elder woman spoke without looking up from her sewing. (She made all her own and Holly's clothes, saving herself pounds and achieving some excellent results.) "Actually he's taken Miss Kent out on the river and I don't imagine he'll be in any great hurry to bring her back. I believe he said something about going out for a drink afterwards."

Peta stared at her incredulously. "He's taken Loriol out? But——"

She had been going to say 'But he didn't say anything to me!' but she caught the words back just in time. She had never been possessive about Mike: if anything it had been the other way round. Instead she said lamely, "I thought Loriol was too busy with Uncle's book to take Mike up on his offer."

Margaret raised her brows. "Don't you know? Your guardian isn't very well, I'm afraid. Apparently the doctor saw him this morning and said that he had been overworking. I gather he's been persuaded to take things more easily for a few days, which means that Miss Kent will have a little more free time." She paused, then added with would-be casualness, "Mike was delighted when she rang up tonight to ask if he could take her out in *Romany*. I really think he's quite smitten by her, though that's hardly surprising, is it? She is extremely attractive."

Mike . . . smitten by Loriol? Peta knitted her brows. What exactly did Mrs. Mandeville mean by that? She surely wasn't seriously suggesting that Mike—no, that would be too silly. He'd never had time for that sort of nonsense!

Margaret Mandeville misinterpreted her silence. She hoped Peta wasn't going to be difficult about this. She herself had been amazed and delighted to find that Loriol Kent's charm and beauty had made such an impression on her graceless son. No one knew better

88

than she that however infatuated he became with the fascinating newcomer, it would never come to anything. Loriol was not the type to become seriously embroiled with someone who still had his way to make in the world. But it would do Mike no harm to adore her for a little while and it would probably do him a great deal of good. He might even come to realise that there were other things in the world beside his wretched boats! And if, at the same time, the friendship between him and Peta suffered, as it was almost bound to do. . !

She saw that there was a look of bewilderment in Peta's eyes and was irritated to feel a pang of compunction. What a child she was . . . what a naïve child! How could she hope to win if her opponent was a girl with the charm and sophistication of Loriol Kent?

She said rather more kindly, "Anyway, there's no need to run away, dear. The children are playing cricket out in the garden: I'm sure they'd like you to join them."

I might be twelve years old! Peta thought indignantly, momentarily forgetting just how many times she *had* joined in Holly's and Dickon's games. Pride made her shake her head.

"I won't stop now, thank you. I'll see Mike some other time: it's not important."

She was about to get back in her car when Holly and Dickon, flushed and dishevelled, came running up to her.

"Peta! Have you seen our ball? Holly's just given it an almighty swipe and it came somewhere in this direction!" Dickon said breathlessly.

Peta looked around her. "Sorry, I didn't notice it, but I've only just come out of the house. Perhaps it went in those bushes over there."

Realising that she was expected to help she joined in the search, and was pushing her way through the laurel bushes when she heard the sound of a car. She stifled a groan. Mike and Loriol! It must be! Oh, bother the beastly ball! If it hadn't been for that she'd have been away by now! At that precise moment she spied it, and emerged from the bushes, holding it triumphantly aloft, just as Mike and Loriol were walking towards the house.

Loriol was wearing a white sweater and navy blue ski pants which showed off her slender, shapely figure to perfection. Her bright hair was wind-tossed and her cheeks glowing. She was laughing up at Mike and there was an expression on his face that Peta did not recognise. Certainly she had never seen it before.

He caught sight of Peta and stopped dead. For a moment he looked dismayed, almost as if he had suddenly been reminded of her existence after forgetting about her for a very long time. Then he recovered, and gave her a somewhat sheepish grin.

"Hullo, old thing! We've just come off the river. Loriol has had her first lesson: shaped jolly well, too!"

"And that, from Mike, is praise indeed, Miss Kent!" Hearing the sound of voices, Margaret Mandeville had emerged from the house and was coming quickly down the path, her eyes watchful in her carefully-composed face.

"Oh, do call her Loriol, Mother! There's no need to stand on ceremony!"

Holly's sharp eyes and ears missed nothing, and she had already arrived at a conclusion of which she disapproved.

"Why didn't you take Peta out on the river as well?" she asked bluntly.

There was an embarrassed silence. Then Mike, his face going red, looked at Peta.

"Sorry, old girl, I suppose I ought to have asked you. But Loriol didn't ring up until late and—well, I'm afraid I just didn't think of it."

"That's all right. I couldn't have come in any case," she said briefly. "I've been visiting someone in hospital. I'm just on my way home now."

"Oh, don't go yet!" Mike said, but he sounded, to Peta's quick ears, only half-hearted.

Baffled and more than a little hurt, she looked at him and shook her head. "I told Ann I wouldn't be late."

Loriol, who had been listening to the little exchange

with a faintly amused expression on her lovely face, stepped forward.

"If you're really going home now would you be kind enough to give me a lift, Peta?" she asked sweetly. Then, as Mike and Mrs. Mandeville protested (rather more convincingly this time), "Yes, I simply must be getting along. I only came back with Mike to collect a book he's promised to lend me."

Why had she been so anxious to go on the river tonight? To punish Nicholas for his neglect? Peta wondered as she started the car. She felt almost sure that that was the kind of thing Loriol *would* do!

For the first time, albeit unwillingly, she tried to conjecture what had happened between Nicholas and Loriol last night after she had gone to bed. Loriol had been seething, there was no doubt about that, and Nicholas . . . well, Nicholas's attitude had hardly been conciliatory. In fact, he had looked at Loriol almost as if he disliked her . . . only of course that was absurd, in view of all the circumstances!

Loriol's voice broke into her thoughts as they left Cedar Lodge behind them, with Mike and Mrs. Mandeville waving from the gate.

"I suppose the someone you mentioned was Richard Mayne? How is he?"

"Better." Peta spoke a little curtly as she skilfully by-passed a lorry. She hadn't really wanted to give Loriol a lift and she didn't feel in the least like a tête-à tête!

Loriol took a cigarette out of her expensive monogrammed handbag and lit it.

"Odd, coming across someone like that in a place like this. In fact, I could hardly believe it when Nicholas told me who he was, though I suppose I shouldn't really have been surprised. He's always had a reputation for eccentricity, I believe."

She blew a cloud of smoke into the air. "I was at school with his daughter, you know. Oh, of course she was a lot older than I was, but I knew her quite well. She was Head Girl during my first two terms."

"His daughter?" In spite of herself Peta spoke sharply. "I didn't know he had one."

Loriol shot her a surprised look. "You mean he hasn't told you about Celia? That's queer. She's his only child: his wife died when she was born and he never married again. Celia was the apple of his eye. She ought to have been terribly spoilt, but she wasn't: nearly everyone liked her."

Peta was silent, willing herself not to pry into Richard's private affairs, but her thoughts were whirling. Why had Richard never mentioned that he had a daughter? He had let her believe that he had no close relatives at all!

She realised that Loriol was still talking about the mysterious Celia.

"Everyone thought she was going to follow in her father's footsteps and become a brilliant artist, but she's married now, I believe, and lives in Paris. I wonder if she knows her father is ill?"

Peta, recognising this as mere idle speculation, refused to be drawn, and Loriol was quickly off on another tack.

"I do hope you don't resent the fact that Mike is teaching me to sail, Peta?"

Oh, that honey-sweetness! It set Peta's teeth on edge, but she contented herself with retorting, "Why should I?"

"Oh, I don't know." A tiny smile curved Loriol's red lips and seeing it, Peta was shaken by sudden anger. She said fiercely, "I don't aspire to own my friends! Mike can do what he likes!"

"How very sensible of you, Peta dear—and, under the circumstances, how fortunate." Loriol sounded lazily amused. "Because, you know, I rather think I shall be needing quite a lot of sailing lessons during the next few days. What with the book held up and Nicholas away, I shall have time on my hands. And I do so hate being bored, don't you?"

It was the second shock Loriol had given her in the space of a few minutes.

"Ni—Dr. Waring is going away?" Why, when he

had told her only last night that he intended to stay?

The long, incredibly thick, gold-tipped lashes flickered. "Unfortunately, yes. Oh, not for long, just for a few days. He's got some urgent business to attend to in London and the Professor wants him to do a bit of research at the British Museum." She paused, then added as if it were a complete afterthought, "I suppose you've realised the way things are between Nicholas and me?"

Peta kept her eyes fixed on the road. They were nearly home now. "I think so, yes."

"We've been in love with each other for ages. As I'm an employee at Greylings at the moment and he's a guest we have to be fairly circumspect, but it's terribly hard, sometimes, to hide what we really feel."

"Why don't you get engaged? Nobody would expect you to hide anything then." Peta was surprised to discover how cool and detached she sounded.

For a moment Loriol seemed slightly taken aback. Then she gave a wry smile.

"I'm afraid it isn't quite as simple as that. Nicholas loves me, but he isn't the marrying kind. He's afraid, I suppose, that a wife will cramp his style, make it impossible for him to lead the kind of life he really likes. I'm having quite a struggle to persuade him to follow his heart and not his head."

She was certainly being frank, Peta thought with some amazement. She did not reply until she had brought the car to a stop outside the front door of Greylings and then she said politely, but with a blatant disregard for truth, "Well, I hope you succeed."

"Oh, I shall," Loriol said lightly. "Don't worry about that. I always get what I want—in the end." She stubbed out her cigarette. "By the way, don't mention this conversation to anyone, will you? Nicholas would be furious if he knew I'd been discussing him."

Peta shook her head and Loriol got out of the car and stood looking down at her with an odd little smile.

"Thanks for the lift. I wondered whether I was taking my life into my hands, but your driving seems to have improved since our first meeting!"

"Cat!" said Peta under her breath, and stuck out her small pink tongue at the retreating back. It was an infantile gesture, but it made her feel a lot better. At least, it did for a minute or two. She found to her surprise that there was a queer little ache in her heart which she'd never experienced before and which she didn't even begin to understand. What was it—plain, simple jealousy? Just because Mike had enjoyed taking a pretty girl out on the river—a girl who by her own admission was practically engaged to somebody else?

"Idiot!" she told herself fiercely, and was dismayed because in spite of there being no valid reason for it to do so, her heart still continued to ache, deaf and blind to reason.

Nicholas left Greylings for London the next day. Peta did not see him alone before he left, but since he said he wanted to make an early start he had breakfast with her and Ann. It was a lovely sunny morning, with billowy white clouds chasing across the sky before a boisterous breeze. Once Peta's spirits would have soared in anticipation of a good day's sailing, but she had slept badly and felt tired and listless.

She felt Nicholas's gaze upon her and wondered if he was noticing the dark stains under her eyes, but all he said was, "How's the patient?"

"Making progress." Peta was surprised to find herself almost tongue-tied, and that was odd, considering how freely she had chatted to him not so very long ago. She added a little shyly, "He asked me to thank you for all that you did for him. And—and he said he'd like to see you, when he comes out of hospital."

"I should like that," Nicholas said promptly. "I admire his work very much. I saw one of his portraits in the Academy a year or two ago—a splendid thing."

Peta stubbed a sandalled foot against the floor. "I know he's made his name as a portrait painter, but he's good at landscapes, too. He's done some marvellous ones since he's been here."

Nicholas laughed. "Well, I expect he was glad of a change. He probably got rather bored with painting a

94

succession of spoiled Society beauties! They all flocked to him at one time, I believe: he could name his own price."

"Anyone else would make him pay fifteen bob an hour. . . ." Peta remembered Mike's words when he had first learned that Richard Mayne was painting her portrait, and she flushed. More than ever it seemed incredible to her that the artist had considered she was worth the effort.

"I must go." Nicholas glanced at his watch and gulped down the last of his coffee. He smiled at Ann as he rose to his feet.

"You make excellent coffee, Miss Devlin. I shall certainly miss your superb cooking during the next few days!"

Ann flushed with pleasure. It was not often that a word of praise or appreciation came her way. She only wished that her brother would occasionally show her a little of the consideration that was so habitual with his younger colleague!

Glancing down, Peta saw that Nicholas had left his briefcase beside his chair, and followed him to the door.

"You've forgotten this." She gave him the briefcase and they stood together for a moment in the early morning sunshine, with a blackbird singing over their heads and Ann's garden a blaze of glory before their eyes. Then Nicholas drew a short breath.

"You know, I'm sorry to leave all this. I've come to the conclusion that only damned fools live in towns! Just look at that sky . . . the colour of that grass . . . those glorious roses!"

"There's a broken one," said Peta prosaically.

Smiling, Nicholas bent and picked it. As he handed it to her their fingers touched and Peta felt her pulse leap as though his life, as well as her own, was flowing through her body. It was an extraordinary sensation, and it almost shook her off balance. For a long moment Nicholas looked down at her, his expression unfathomable, then he said abruptly, "Loriol tells me that Mike is teaching her how to sail."

95

It was such a bewildering change of subject that Peta stared.

"Yes." Something, some innate sense of fairness, made her add, "He says she's shaping very well."

He frowned. "I don't doubt it. But——" He stopped, and Peta had the impression he was searching for the right words. Then he gave a little shrug, as if he had given up the attempt, and said lightly, "Say goodbye to the Professor for me, won't you? Au revoir, Peta."

Watching him go, Peta wondered where and when he had said goodbye to Loriol . . . and what he had been going to say a few moments ago. It had been something about Loriol, she was sure of that. Her brows knit together in a little frown. Surely Nicholas wasn't jealous? Not of Mike! That would be too silly for words!

But certainly Loriol, in the days that followed, showed no sign of pining away. The weather was fine and sunny, and since her evenings were now completely free she spent most of them on the river with Mike. The latter made a point, at first, of asking Peta to accompany them, but when she explained that she was tied up with her visits to the hospital she had a feeling that he was secretly relieved. It was natural enough, she told herself angrily: three was an awkward number. Mike himself had said, before Loriol's arrival, that two was company and three was none. Only she hadn't really expected that she, Peta, would ever be the odd one out!

It was typical of her that although she realised that Loriol had temporarily, at least, ousted her from her place in Mike's friendship, she grieved only for the loss of the old perfect comradeship between them. She didn't blame him for being fascinated by Loriol's golden beauty, but it hurt intolerably that she had been so completely set aside. Innately loyal herself, his fickleness was incomprehensible to her—especially as she knew quite well that Loriol didn't really want him, she was merely making use of him. When Nicholas returned, she thought, Mike would tumble to that fact too—and then perhaps it would be his turn to feel hurt and bewildered.

In the meantime there *was* someone who needed her and looked forward to her company—Richard Mayne. She went to see him every evening, the only visitor who was ever admitted to the little white cubicle where he was slowly recovering from the heart attack that had nearly killed him.

His loneliness had always worried Peta, but now that she knew of the existence of his daughter she was haunted day and night by the riddle of his silence concerning her. What had happened to cause him to cut a much-loved child—'the apple of his eye,' Loriol had described her—so completely out of his life that even when he was seriously ill he did not want her near him?

She wished she knew the answer, not because she was inquisitive but because she somehow felt convinced that it was the key to the artist's present depression. To ask him outright about Celia, or attempt to force his confidence, would take more courage than she possessed, she thought. Questions were intrusive and she had always believed that what people did not tell you about themselves was none of your business.

Yet there came an evening when she let Richard know that she had learnt of Celia's existence. He had been talking, with rather more animation than usual, of what had apparently been his favourite sport—skiing.

"You must try it one day, my dear," he told her. "I have never found anything else quite so exhilarating. We used to spend part of every winter in Switzerland: we never missed for years and years."

"We?" Peta looked up, her heart suddenly thudding against her ribs as she decided to take the bull by the horns. "Oh, I suppose you mean you and Celia."

There was a moment's silence. Peta, forcing herself to meet his suddenly inimical gaze, saw that he had gone very pale and that all the contours of his face had become painfully sharpened.

"Who told you about Celia?" There was a harshness in his voice she had never heard before.

She answered him quietly, "Loriol Kent, my guardian's secretary. She said she was at school with your daughter."

There was another silence. Then the artist said, still in the same harsh voice, "Well, I suppose you're wondering why I've never mentioned her. I may as well tell you that Celia doesn't belong in my life any more. We quarrelled bitterly four years ago. We've both got hot tempers, we both said things to each other that were unforgivable. In the end I told her that if—that if she took a certain step I never wanted to see or hear from her again, and she knew I meant what I said." He stopped, his expression brooding.

Peta looked at him, nearly as pale as he. *"Then* perhaps you did. But now. . . ."

"Now that I'm on the way out, you mean?" Ignoring her shocked protest, he gave a hard laugh. "Do you think I want my daughter's pity? Oh, I'd get it all right if she knew I was ill: she always was one for lame dogs." He paused for a moment and his mouth twisted into a bitter smile.

"Ironically enough, ever since I've known you I've had regrets about what happened. You aren't really like Celia, and yet you've made me realise how much I miss my own girl. The day I had this blasted attack I received a letter from her. It was the third time she'd written, but I sent the other two letters back unopened. This time I—well, I couldn't do it. I read what she had to say, and I must say it shook me up. I could think of nothing else all day. I—I think I might even have had said yes, let bygones be bygones, if *this* hadn't happened." He cast a look of loathing round the small white cubicle. "Do you think I want her to find me like this? An object for compassion?"

Peta caught her breath. "But it wouldn't make any difference! Oh, Mr. Mayne, please answer her letter!"

"No. Not now," he said curtly, and there was such a note of finality in his voice that she dared not argue. She longed to tell him what she thought of his stubborn pride, but in spite of it all her heart ached for his unhappiness and for the quarrel which had spoilt what must have been a relationship he'd prized.

She was rather afraid that her own friendship with the artist might now be affected, but on her next visit to the hospital Celia was not mentioned and Richard seemed to be in slightly better spirits. He wanted, he told her, to give a birthday present to the Sister who had been particularly kind to him, and he asked her if the next time she came she would bring with her his cheque book. He thought she would find it in a drawer in his bedroom.

In point of fact it wasn't there, but she eventually found it half-hidden among a pile of papers on a small table in his studio. That sort of carelessness was typical, she thought with a shake of her head. She extracted the cheque book from beneath a dog-eared portfolio and as she did so she accidentally knocked some papers to the ground. A photograph fluttered out of a long blue envelope and she picked it up. It was an informal snapshot of a pretty girl with a fresh, happy face, a good-looking young man, and two tiny boys with curly hair and engaging smiles. On the back was a simple inscription—'From Celia.'

Celia! Peta's eyes widened. So this was Richard Mayne's daughter—and the good-looking man must be her husband and the two little boys their children! They looked darlings. Oh, how could Richard bear not to know them?

Instinctively she looked at the envelope, which bore a Paris postmark. This must be the letter to which Richard had referred!—the one he had received the day he had had his heart attack! It bore the address of a London club, and had been forwarded on. She turned it over. The name of the sender—Mrs. Celia Montel—and her address were clearly written on the back.

She sighed, and was about to replace the photograph and put the envelope back on the table, with its litter of books and papers, when a wild idea suddenly occurred to her. Richard Mayne was too proud to write to his daughter, but supposing . . . just supposing . . . she, Peta, wrote instead? It was a frightful gamble, and probably when he found out he'd never ever forgive her for her interference. But Richard was eating his heart out and if there was even a slight chance that her letter might bring him and his daughter together again . . . wasn't it worth the risk? She drew a deep breath. Seizing a pencil, she hurriedly copied out the name and address on a scrap of paper. She had made up her mind that she would write to Celia that very night.

CHAPTER SEVEN

IT seemed to Peta during the next few days that her life had never been so full of problems and complications at it was now. It would have been bad enough if she'd only had Mike's involvement with Loriol and the letter she'd sent to Celia Montel to worry about, but even at Greylings the previous halcyon calm had been rudely shattered.

Professor Devlin, depressed and irritable because he did not feel well enough to proceed with his book as fast as he would have liked, was at his most difficult. He found fault with everyone and everything, but almost inevitably Peta was the chief target for his caustic tongue. They had several heated arguments, mainly about her job, though it seemed as though everything she said and did was a source of irritation. Belatedly she began to realise how much they had owed to Nicholas, and how far his unfailing tact and pleasant manners had gone to ensure the untroubled atmosphere of the past weeks.

Now that she was no longer blinded by hurt pride and prejudice she also recognised the many occasions when, unobtrusively but effectively, he had acted as a kind of buffer between her and her guardian. Now there was no one, for Ann always found it hard to stand up to her brother and Loriol seemed to find the endless arguments amusing. Indeed, Peta was almost sure that whenever she could she added fuel to the flames. Certainly it was her seemingly innocent suggestion that Peta should learn to type and do shorthand which sparked off a particularly acrimonious wrangle.

"Since you apparently have no desire for any form of higher education, Miss Kent's idea seems to me to be admirable." Professor Devlin spoke coldly, annoyed by Peta's horrified reaction. "It is perfectly obvious that you cannot remain at that absurd sailing school. The job is completely unsuitable in every way."

"I don't see why." Peta's eyes sparkled with indigna-

101

tion. "I don't earn much, I know, but it's enough to keep me and—and I'm *happy*! Isn't that important? I couldn't bear to be cooped up in a stuffy office!"

"Perhaps because you might be called upon to do some *real* work," her guardian said bitingly. "It is about time, Peta, that you realised that life is not a playground, and that you did not receive an expensive education merely to enable you to fritter away your time sailing a boat!"

It was hardly to be expected that Peta would take that kind of remark lying down. The argument raged, and would have probably continued to rage for some time had Loriol not intervened.

"I'm sorry the idea of shorthand and typing doesn't appeal," she said, smiling blandly at Peta. "I was only trying to help. I thought, you know, that you'd need to find something else to do during the winter. The sailing school *will* close at the end of the season, won't it?"

Her words gave Peta an unpleasant jolt. She had never been one to let thoughts of tomorrow spoil her enjoyment of today, but for the first time she forced herself to face up to the fact that at the end of September she would almost certainly find herself in a very awkward position. She would have to look around for another job to tide her over until next spring—but what? And whatever it was, unless it was some kind of solid career her guardian was almost bound to disapprove!

It was a problem that later she talked over with Richard Mayne. Greatly to her chagrin she found that he had a certain amount of sympathy with the Professor's viewpoint.

"I don't think you're wasting your time, exactly, but I do think that perhaps you're wasting your opportunities," he said gently. "Must you stay here, in Norfolk? It's a large world, my dear. Why not see what another corner of it has to offer?"

Peta shook her head. "Wild horses wouldn't make me leave Norfolk! It's home."

"H'm. Is it that young Viking of yours who's holding

you here?" Richard asked, with rather more bluntness than usual.

The colour flamed into Peta's face and she turned her head away. Richard, in hospital, did not know of Mike's defection. He seemed to be the only person who didn't. The village gossips, she knew, were already busy, and not without reason. Mike had never been seen with any girl except her, so that obviously the amount of time he was now spending in Loriol's company was provoking comment. Nobody, as yet, had dared to say anything to her, but she was aware of sympathetic glances and even the Norwells, with rather heavy tact, refrained from mentioning Mike's name.

Before she could answer Richard a nurse came in to give him some pills, but she was still thinking about what he had said about 'wasted opportunities' when she went home. In fact, she was so absorbed in thought as she let herself into the house that it was not until she was halfway across the hall that she noticed the tall figure descending the stairs.

"Hello, Peta."

Nicholas! She stood stockstill, her face irradiated. She had not known he was coming back today and for a moment she was speechless with surprise and pleasure.

He was smiling as he came towards her, but it struck her that there was tension in the way he held his shoulders. It was as though he was keeping some sort of curb on himself.

"I'm almost tempted to delude myself that you're glad to see me!" he said lightly, and she imagined that she saw the amusement at the back of his eyes.

She flushed and laughed and answered him with the same lightness.

"Well, of course I am! Why didn't you let us know you were coming?" Something made her add, "I expect Loriol is out, isn't she?"

Nicholas's brows lifted the fraction of an inch and something flickered behind his eyes.

"Yes, she is. Miss Devlin tells me that her enthusiasm for sailing is unbounded!"

There was a certain amount of dryness in his voice, but Peta was saved from answering by the appearance of Ann.

"John would like to see you in the library, Dr. Waring, if that's all right? I expect he wants to start work immediately on the material you've unearthed for him, but you won't let him, will you? He's already done far more than he ought today."

"No, I'll make him wait until tomorrow," Nicholas promised her, and he was as good as his word. After about half an hour he left the Professor alone with his books and joined Ann and Peta, who were enjoying an interval of blessed peace in the drawing room. There hadn't been many such intervals during Nicholas's absence: John Devlin had seen to that!

Ann was writing a letter. Nicholas settled himself in a fireside chair opposite Peta and relaxed with what might have been a sigh of content.

"I must be getting old. London's hurly-burly is too much for me: the pace seems to get more and more hectic all the time."

Peta, who was sitting on a stool hugging her knees, looked up at him.

"Did you do all that you wanted to do? Loriol said you had some urgent business to attend to."

He did not answer her for a moment. Then he said slowly, "In some ways it was a successful trip. I found out all the Professor wanted to know: that part was all right. I haven't been able to make up my mind what to do about my own affairs, though, I need a little longer to think things over."

"I shouldn't have thought you were the sort of person to be troubled with indecision!"

A slightly rueful smile touched his lips. "I'm not, as a rule. But this is a question of what I'm going to do with myself for the next two or three years. I've been invited, you see, to join an archaeological team which is going out to South America later this year to carry on, more or less, where the Professor and I had to leave off. In actual fact I'm very keen to return to that part of the world and I've got one or two theories that I think

104

might be worth following up. But. . . ." he hesitated.

Ann, whose attention had been divided between her letter and what he was saying, laid down her pen.

"I don't quite understand the problem. If it's what you want to do. . . ."

Nicholas was frowning down at the glowing tip of his cigarette. "I know. But it's not quite as simple as it seems. There are—certain complications," he said quietly, and though Ann still looked puzzled, Peta understood.

Loriol was the complication. Would she want to go back to South America? Unlikely . . . she'd said again and again that she'd disliked Peru and that she wanted to settle somewhere in Europe. Preferably London, which judging by his remarks Nicholas hated. But which would be the stronger, his love for his work or his love for Loriol? What would he do, in the end . . . follow his heart or his head?

She looked at the clock. Loriol was late tonight, later than she had ever been. Suddenly she knew that she couldn't bear to sit around and wait until she came home. She didn't want to see Nicholas's face light up when she came into the room. It was silly . . . petty . . . but there it was.

Later, lying in bed, she heard eleven o'clock strike and still Loriol had not arrived home. Nicholas must be waiting up for her, for though Ann had come upstairs she had not heard anyone else pass her door. She turned her head restlessly on the pillow. Why was Loriol so late? and how would she react when she found that Nicholas had returned to Greylings so unexpectedly? One thing was for sure, she'd have no more time for Mike. He'd be out in the cold, unwanted.

The thought ought to have given Peta satisfaction, but it didn't. She didn't want Mike to be hurt. She also knew, with a sense of desolation, that whatever happened it was unlikely that their friendship would ever be the same again. Loriol had come between them, and even when she'd gone her shadow would remain.

An owl hooted somewhere in the garden and the wind surged in the trees. Melancholy sounds, both. A little later she heard the sound of a car, but by that time she was so nearly asleep that the noise only just registered. Her last conscious thought was of Mike, but oddly it was of Nicholas she dreamt. At least, it was Nicolas to begin with, but when she awoke it was with a confused impression that in one rather jumbled-up dream Mike, Loriol, she and even the Mandeville children had all played a part.

She remembered that dream when the next evening Mike telephoned to say that his mother thought that a picnic by the sea might be a pleasant way of spending Sunday afternoon.

"I've already mentioned it to Loriol and she's very keen. We'll go to Horsey, of course: I know it's a long walk to the beach, but at least it isn't as crowded as everywhere else. You will come, won't you, Peta?"

The invitation gave Peta a little shock of pleasure. Here was proof, she thought remorsefully, that Mike still cared about her friendship, Loriol or no Loriol! She had no way of knowing that at first neither Margaret Mandeville nor Mike had considered it necessary to include her in their plans. It was Dickon and Holly who had protested indignantly when they had discovered that Peta wasn't being asked, and for the sake of peace and quiet Margaret had given in.

"I'd love to come," Peta answered Mike with something akin to her old eagerness. Then she hesitated. "I suppose Loriol said yes, too? What—what about Nicholas? He came back last night, you know."

"Oh, did he?" Mike's voice did not sound enthusiastic. "Well, I suppose he'd better come along as well."

He hesitated in his turn, then added awkwardly, "I hope Loriol's headache is better?"

"Her headache?"

"Yes. She rang Mum up this afternoon and said she didn't feel well enough to go on the river tonight. It's a pity, I don't suppose this fine weather will last much longer."

Mike spoke with careful nonchalance, but Peta was conscious of a spurt of wild anger. There was nothing wrong with Loriol! She'd been laughing and talking to

106

Nicholas all through dinner and directly it was over they had gone out somewhere together. Oh, why were men such idiots? Why couldn't Mike, steady, sensible Mike, see right through her?

For a moment she was strongly tempted to tell him the truth. Then she bit back the angry words and answered him briefly.

"I don't know how she is. I haven't seen much of her tonight. I've got to go now, Mike: I'm helping Ann with the washing up. There's too much for her to do alone."

She put the receiver down without even giving Mike a chance to say goodbye and went back to the kitchen, her lips tightly compressed. Just at that moment she felt as though she almost hated Loriol: Mike was too good a sort to be lied to. It seemed as though he was living in some kind of fool's Paradise, but if so it wasn't likely to last much longer. If Nicholas came to the picnic on Sunday Mike would surely see for himself which way the wind was blowing. There seemed to be no reason, now, why Loriol shouldn't make her preference plain.

She discovered, to her amazement, that she had never been more wrong.

The day of the picnic broke still and clear as heart could wish. There had been so long a spell of real summer that everyone had fallen into the habit of expecting good weather and Mrs. Mandeville had made her plans without any qualms. She, Mike, Holly and Dickon travelled to Horsey in Mike's car and joined up with Peta, Nicholas and Loriol on the beach, which, because it was better known to locals than to ordinary holidaymakers, was practically deserted. The sand was soft and warm under their feet, and the waves rolled on the beach and broke into a rustle of foam.

"Goodness, doesn't that water look inviting?" said Loriol gaily. "I do wish I could swim, I'd be in there like a shot!" for oddly enough it appeared that among her various accomplishments she did not number swimming.

"Oh, we'll soon put that right!" Mike said eagerly.

"I'll teach you to swim in no time. I'm certain you won't have any difficulty—you grasp things so quickly."

"If you're thinking of my prowess on the river there's as much credit due to the teacher as to the pupil!" said Loriol. Laughing up at him, she reached out an apparently careless hand and wound it round his in a gesture of intimacy.

Peta blinked. Instinctively she glanced at Nicholas, but his brown face was impassive. It was always hard to tell what he was thinking, but surely he didn't care for Loriol to be on quite such good terms with Mike?

Puzzled and perturbed, she turned away to organise a game of cricket for Holly and Dickon. Usually she and Mike bathed together, for they were like a pair of fishes in the sea and had perfected a number of aquatic antics. Today, however, Mike was entirely taken up with teaching Loriol to swim and had eyes for nobody else. Not that that was really surprising: Loriol looked wonderful in a swim-suit and even with a bathing cap hiding her beautiful hair her laughing face was most attractive.

"Aren't you going in?" Holly looked at Peta.

"Later, after lunch, perhaps." Peta forced herself to speak lightly and took the bat that Dickon was holding to her. Nicholas was bowling: he too, apparently, felt no desire to bathe yet awhile. Yet if anyone was going to teach Loriol to swim, shouldn't it have been him?

Herself incapable of any form of pretence or subterfuge, she felt more and more bewildered as the day wore on. Loriol was practically ignoring Nicholas's existence and devoting herself almost exclusively to Mike. In fact, Peta thought, she was flirting outrageously, with a blatant disregard for what anyone thought. But why? What was she trying to prove?

The disturbing thought came to her that perhaps, for some extraordinary reason of her own, Loriol was trying to make Nicholas jealous. If so the plan did not appear to be succeeding very well: he seemed totally unconcerned. If she did not know better she might even have been fooled into thinking he did not care.

Margaret Mandeville, lying back in a deckchair, was

watching the two with a little smile lifting the corner of her lips. She was obviously quite happy about the situation, although the same could hardly be said of Dickon and Holly. The former was annoyed because Mike was so absorbed in Loriol that he had no time for cricket, and Holly was furious on Peta's behalf. Mike was *her* boy-friend and always had been! What right had he to chase after anyone else, however beautiful she was? She thought she knew just how Peta was feeling and tried, clumsily, to show her sympathy by being especially affectionate. At the same time she treated Loriol in an offhand manner which almost verged on rudeness, and which more than once brought a frown to her mother's face.

Peta appreciated the child's loyalty, but was terrified that she might precipitate a 'scene'. Her own feelings were extraordinarily confused. She was torn between exasperation with Mike, bewilderment at Loriol's attitude and sympathy for Nicholas. He was in the same boat as herself. What did he really think of Loriol's behaviour? And why was she being so capricious? What could possibly have gone wrong between her and Nicholas since his return from London?

For her, lunch was an uncomfortable meal, for she was not hungry and could manage to eat very little of the good fare provided. Luckily no one commented on the fact, though once she looked up to find Nicholas studying her intently. That worried her a little. She did not want him to guess how unhappy she was feeling and immediately became unusually talkative.

After lunch Holly proposed a walk along the bleak, windswept coast. Everyone fell in with her suggestion except her mother, who said firmly that she drew the line at violent exercise after eating. Peta would have preferred to have stayed with her, but dared not say so, it would have seemed too odd.

They started off as a group but almost inevitably they soon separated into pairs, with Mike and Loriol leading the way, Nicholas and Dickon following and Peta and Holly bringing up the rear. It was too hot to go very fast and Peta, in particular, was handicapped by a broken sandal strap, which made progress along the loose, shifting sand ten times more difficult. In the end she took her shoes off and walked barefoot. She didn't want to lag behind, though she wasn't enjoying herself a bit. Instead of making an effort to appear gay and light-hearted it would have been wonderful to be alone, and to hear only the sound of the sea and the gulls calling to one another as they wheeled over the water.

"I do think Mike is horrid! And you're silly, Peta, you really are!" Holly waited until a moment when she judged she and Peta were out of earshot of the others and let her pent-up indignation break out.

Peta's heart missed a beat. She had hoped that Holly had been deceived by the nonsense she had been talking and that she had managed to convey the idea that all was well and there was nothing remarkable about the situation at all.

"What *are* you talking about?" she asked with assumed obtuseness.

"Oh, don't pretend, Peta! You and Mike, of course!" Holly looked at her with wide, indignant eyes. "Why are you letting Loriol snaffle him? He belongs to you, not her!"

"Don't talk like that!" Peta said, sharply for her. "Mike doesn't 'belong' to anyone, and certainly not to me. Why shouldn't he have other friends if he wants them? Of course he finds Loriol attractive, anyone would!"

Holly kicked at a stone. "It's not fair on you!"

"Now it's you who's being silly! I don't mind in the least."

She hoped she sounded convincing, but was doubtful, for after all she *did* mind, for a variety of reasons.

Holly's next words took her completely by surprise.

"That's a fib, but I don't blame you for telling it. I blame Mike. He's too thick to see that Loriol is just playing about, she'll drop him like a hot potato when she feels like it." She sighed. "I suppose you won't still marry him, after this?"

Peta, already stunned by the child's astuteness, could only gape.

"*Marry* him?"

"Oh, I know you haven't thought much about it yet." Holly gave her a quick sidelong glance. "Mum was furious when I mentioned it, she said you were just good friends. I didn't argue with her, but of course anyone can see you were just made for each other." Holly, who read every woman's magazine she could lay her hands on, spoke with her most grown-up air. "I expect you'd soon have realised that for yourself, if Loriol hadn't come and messed things up for everyone!"

Just at that moment Dickon shouted to his sister to come and see something he'd found, and for a few seconds, until she caught them up, Peta was left alone to wrestle with an entirely new thought.

She had laughed to scorn any suggestion that Mike might be anything but her very good friend and companion—but was Holly right? Would she, in time, have woken up to the realisation that he was very much more? Was that why she'd not only been feeling hurt and a little resentful, but also heartsore, these last few days?

She wrinkled her brow in perplexity. Unlike Holly, she didn't pretend to know the first thing about love, but she'd always imagined that there must be something rather searing and electrifying about the real thing. Perhaps, though, romance did not always come into one's life with pomp and blare, like a gay knight riding down . . . perhaps, sometimes, it just unfolded naturally out of a beautiful friendship. Perhaps she and Mike. . . .

Absorbed in her thoughts, she did not notice where she was walking and the next moment she let out an involuntary cry of pain as a piece of broken glass with a sharp, jagged edge, which had been left protruding out of the sand, gashed her bare foot. It was a bad cut, and by the time the rest of the party had come running back to see what had happened the handkerchief she had quickly wrapped round it was soaked with blood.

"Let me see." Nicholas knelt down on the sand beside her and gently took her foot in his hands. His lips tightened as he inspected the damage. "H'm. A nasty cut, my child. You'll need a dressing on that."

"Why on earth weren't you wearing your sandals?" Loriol demanded coldly.

"A strap broke." Feeling thoroughly fed up and annoyed with herself, Peta spoke shakily. "I didn't see the glass."

"I say! It's bleeding jolly badly!" Dickon's eyes were on the reddening sand. "You'll have to go back to the car, Peta. Mum always keeps a first aid box in the back, she'll soon fix you up."

"Yes, but she can't walk, not on that!" Holly protested. "Somebody will have to carry her," and she looked straight at her brother.

There was a moment's painful silence. A slow flush crept up under Mike's tan, but he said nothing.

"Oh, I don't think it's as bad as all that, is it?" Loriol, who was holding on to his arm, sounded both bored and impatient, and Peta, in an agony of embarrassment, tried to scramble to her feet.

"Of course it isn't—" she began, but Nicholas cut her short. Before she realised what he intended to do he had swung her up in his arms as easily as if she had been a child, ignoring both her horrified protests and the expression on Loriol's face.

"Holly's quite right, you can't walk on a cut like that. I'll carry you, it's not far."

He began walking back in the direction from which they had come, bearing her weight without any apparent effort.

"Oh, please put me down!" Peta, her feelings now indescribable, was near to tears. Such a stupid accident, and it had spoiled the walk for Nicholas—and the last thing in the world she wanted was to be held in his arms like this, as if she really were the silly child he'd once called her!

"I'm much too heavy, you'll feel like dropping me in the sea long before we get back to the car!"

Nicholas laughed, "Heavy? You're a feather-weight, my child." He paused, then added deliberately, "Not that I'm surprised. I've noticed that you seem to have lost your appetite recently."

The colour rushed into Peta's pale cheeks and she gave a nervous little laugh.

"It's been too hot to eat."

For a long moment he looked down into the face against his shoulder, then he said, with a gentleness which made tears sting her eyelids, "That's not the only reason. It's Mike, isn't it?"

Only ten minutes ago Peta would have denied his suggestion vehemently. Now, confused and bewildered, she was still struggling to discover the secrets of her own heart and so she did not answer.

He took her silence for consent and she saw his lips twist. Of course, she thought with a pang, it's horrid for him, too. Even though he must know Loriol isn't serious about Mike he's got a right to expect very different behaviour from the girl he intends to make his wife!

She said a little desperately, trying to console him, "Everyone knows that—that Loriol isn't really serious."

"No?" He gave an odd little laugh. "And Mike? What about him?"

She swallowed. Jogging a little as he walked, their cheeks touched, and she could feel his warm breath.

"I think—I think it's just that he's never met anyone like Loriol before. She's bowled him over."

Looking up into his face, she saw that it was sombre.

"Yes, she does have that effect. I'm sorry, my dear. I—I wish there was something I could do about it."

There was a note in his voice she did not understand. Puzzled, she nearly said, "But there is. The moment you and Loriol announce your engagement Mike will know that she wasn't in earnest." She choked the words back, but it wasn't only because she suddenly remembered her promise to Loriol. Somehow she just couldn't bring herself to talk about something she found so wholly unpalatable.

Instead she said a little chokingly, "Thank you, anyway, for—for understanding." The moment she'd said it she realised that perhaps she was giving a false

113

impression and searched around in her mind for a more appropriate word, but Nicholas seemed to find nothing wrong with it.

He was smiling faintly, and she thought the smile was tinged with bitterness.

" 'A fellow feeling makes one wond'rous kind'. Don't worry, my dear. It will probably all work out in the end, if that's any comfort." Then, with a quick change of manner and tone, "Well, here we are and here's Mrs. Mandeville coming to meet us. Do you think you could possibly summon up a wave and a bright brave smile? The good lady looks positively alarmed!"

Margaret did, indeed, look worried. "Peta, what on earth have you done to yourself?"

"Only gashed my foot on a piece of broken glass. I'm sure it looks much worse than it really is, but Nicholas wouldn't let me walk on it."

Peta, feeling horribly self-conscious, was glad when Nicholas put her gently down on the sand and went to fetch the first aid box from Margaret's car. Her foot was aching badly and so was her head, a little, but what was worse was that though she didn't know why, misery seemed to have settled like a ball of lead just below the base of her throat. She had never felt more utterly dejected and she had to fight against an absurd desire to cry.

When the cut had been carefully cleansed and bandaged by Margaret's skilful hands she begged so hard to be left alone that eventually she was allowed to have her own way. Margaret and Nicholas strolled off to meet the others and she was left by herself, with only the roar of the breakers and the shrill cries of the seagulls to distract her from the confused and weary circling of her thoughts.

114

CHAPTER EIGHT

LORIOL did not leave Peta in any doubts as to the reason for her treament of Nicholas. She came to her bedroom late that night, ostensibly to enquire if her foot was comfortable, though even Peta was not naïve enough to believe for one moment that this was her real purpose.

She tapped lightly at the door, which was ajar.

"May I come in?"

"I suppose so." For the life of her Peta could not help sounding ungracious and Loriol's brows rose a little. She advanced towards the bed, slender and graceful in an exquisite silk negligée with ruffles of lace and chiffon, and perched herself on the edge of the mattress. Her eyes were wide and amused. In her faded cotton pyjamas, with her hair tied back in a pony-tail, Peta looked younger—and more vulnerable—than ever.

"Don't look so suspicious! I've only come to ask how your foot is."

Peta felt like saying that she hadn't seemed unduly concerned about it earlier, but contented herself with a curt "Better, thanks."

"I'm glad." Loriol made herself comfortable and let her gaze wander round the small, bare room. Perhaps, to nearly everyone else who knew Peta, the room would have been suggestive of the girl's free spirit, so extraordinarily indifferent to possessions of any kind, but Loriol was puzzled and even a little affronted by its touch of austerity.

"You're a queer child, Peta. You don't go in for 'pretties' very much, do you?"

"If by 'pretties' you mean frills and furbelows, then no, I don't." Peta picked up the book which she had laid aside as Loriol had entered, and hoped that she would take the hint.

Loriol's eyes narrowed a little, but she laughed.

"You're not very sociable tonight, are you? What's the matter?"

"Nothing."

Loriol laughed again. "You don't expect me to believe that, do you? You know quite well you're feeling sore about Mike. I suppose you think I'm a beast, but you needn't hate me, you know. You can have him back—when he's served his purpose."

The sheer arrogance of this remark almost took Peta's breath away. She stared incredulously at the elder girl, wondering if she had heard aright.

"What do you mean?"

"Just what I say." Loriol studied her long, pointed fingernails with exaggerated care. "I rather hoped, in view of the little heart-to-heart we had recently, that you would have had more sense than to be taken in by today's little charade. No, let me finish!" as Peta, fury in her eyes, started to interrupt. "You know perfectly well I don't want Mike Mandeville! He's a nice boy, but he *is* a boy, and I'm only interested in men. No, one man, Nicholas."

"Then you've got a jolly funny way of showing it!" Peta's voice shook and there was a high spot of colour in each of her cheeks. She was beginning to feel that she was in some kind of a bad dream.

"Not really." A faint smile curled Loriol's lip and if she saw the scorn in Peta's face she took no notice. "Nicholas, you see, is taking rather too long to make up his mind that he can't live without me. I object to being kept dangling at the end of a piece of string, so I thought that a little jolt in the shape of a reminder that he's not the only pebble on my beach would do him no harm at all. It doesn't do to let men take you for granted—particularly men like Dr. Nicholas Waring!"

"You mean you admit that you're deliberately trying to make him jealous? Just using Mike to suit your own ends?" Peta's face flamed, and she added in a low, passionate voice, "I think you're a—a snake! Don't you care how much you hurt people? What about Mike? He—he's serious about you!"

"That's just too bad." Loriol's little shrug was almost contemptuous. "At his age he should know the differ-

116

ence between a light-hearted flirtation and the real thing."

It was only with a tremendous effort that Peta controlled her temper. She said hotly, "Well, you may find that you've been just a bit too clever! Nicholas doesn't strike me as the sort of person you can play fast and loose with! It would serve you right if you lost him altogether! He—he's much too good for you, anyway!"

"Frank, if hardly flattering!" Loriol mocked. She laughed, and there was suddenly something in her face which was hard and ugly. "What an infant you are, Peta! Don't be fooled just because Nicholas decided to play knight errant today! He probably sized up the situation between Mike and me and decided that two could play the same game!"

Peta felt suddenly sick. "Get out!" she said between clenched teeth, and with another of those infuriating little shrugs Loriol got up and sauntered towards the door.

Alone, Peta turned her face into her pillow, almost unable to believe, despite the evidence of her own ears, that anyone could be so ruthless with such cool deliberation. How could either Mike or Nicholas, both such *genuine* people, fall in love with someone like that? She set her lips grimly. She could do nothing about Nicholas, but Mike was her oldest friend, she could and would try to do something to try to open *his* eyes! She simply couldn't stand by and watch Loriol make a fool of him any longer!

These thoughts chased each other around in her head far into the night and when at last she fell asleep she had made up her mind to have things out with Mike at the first opportunity. This, however, was easier said than done, and in the meantime she found it impossible to decide whether Loriol's tactics were having the desired effect on Nicholas or not. He was, of course, a hard nut to crack. Apart from the fact that he was obviously not sure whether there was any place for a permanent partner in his life, he was not the kind of man to allow love to make him either humble or supplicating. His manner towards Loriol, in public at least, was exactly the same as it had always been. Polite and pleasant. Under his calm exterior, however, Peta felt reasonably sure that he must be smouldering, for Loriol's behaviour was nothing if not inflammatory. She seemed to be doing her level best, by means of her flirtation with Mike, to provoke him into some kind of passionate declaration and Peta could only guess at her chagrin when nothing happened.

For her part she felt oddly shy of Nicholas and avoided him as much as possible. She told herself that this was because he thought she was eating her heart out for Mike, and she did not want his pity, however kindly meant.

What was it he'd said? 'A fellow feeling makes one wond'rous kind.' That was all very well, but she didn't really know whether they did, in fact, share a fellow feeling! Was the hurt she felt at Mike's defection, her indignation on his behalf, love . . . the real thing? How could she possibly know? Since that afternoon on the beach she'd tried so many times to analyse her feelings for Mike, but she'd never got very far. The queer thing was that every time she started to recall the many hours she'd spent with him, walking, sailing and riding, other and newer memories kept intruding. It was, of course, completely coincidental that Nicholas played a major role in these, but it was also frustrating. Love, she decided gloomily, was obviously the nuisance she'd always thought it. It just brought problems, nothing else.

She tried several times to see Mike alone, but never succeeded. If she called at his home he was always out with Loriol: if she telephoned it was always Margaret who answered, and she invariably said that Mike was not available. She was so distant on these occasions that at last Peta got the message: she was being warned off. So even Mike's mother, she thought unhappily, had been taken in by Loriol's facile charm.

Tired and dispirited, her morale was at low ebb when at lunchtime on Saturday she was amazed to find Mike waiting for her by the boathouse.

"Mike! Where have you sprung from?"

Realising that Stephen Norwell might be within ear-shot she tried not to look and sound too surprised, but she saw Mike flush.

"Long time no see, you mean?" He gave an uneasy laugh. "Sorry, old thing. I suppose I have been neglecting you rather badly."

"Oh, don't apologise!" Peta forced herself to speak lightly. "I've been pretty well tied up myself just lately. I go to see Mr. Mayne every night, you know: there isn't anyone else and he always seems glad to see me."

"Yes, Loriol told me you'd more or less adopted the old boy."

There was a little silence, then he added awkwardly, "Well, how's life?"

"Oh, fine, thanks." Was this really *Mike* she was talking to? This stiff stranger? They'd be exchanging remarks about the weather next, she thought, and had to suppress a hysterical desire to giggle.

Mike ran his fingers through his hair. He seemed horribly ill at ease.

"Look, Peta, can we sit down somewhere and talk for a minute? I—well, there's something I want to ask you about next week."

Of course, Peta thought, the regatta! In spite of everything her spirits lifted. However dazzled he was by Loriol's charm and beauty, he wouldn't be able to do without her, Peta, next weekend! Perhaps, just for one afternoon, they would be able to regain their old friendly footing . . . be comrades again!

Her face lighting up, she said eagerly, "About the regatta, you mean? Have you found out yet who'll be competing in our class?"

"No. No, I haven't." Mike stuck his hands in his pockets. Looking anywhere but at her he said uncomfortably, "Look—I don't quite know how to say this, but would you mind very much if—if you didn't sail with me next Saturday?"

"Not sail with you?" Peta echoed the words blankly. "But why? What's the matter? Is there anything wrong with *Romany*?"

"Of course not." Mike drew a deep breath. "It's—

well, it's Loriol. She's absolutely crazy to do a bit of real racing. I thought—if she came with me in *Romany* . . . you could crew for Sam Merridew. I—I know he's looking for someone, his sister broke her leg last week."

Down by the landing-stage two small dinghies were bobbing and curtseying, rubbing each other's shoulders as the water lapped at them with soft sucking sounds. Someone had been peeling an orange, and Peta stood watching the lift and fall of the spinning fragments as they drifted along the surface. Presently she said, "You mean you don't want me to crew for you, you want Loriol?"

"There's no need to put it quite like that." Mike had been watching her face and now he spoke defensively, almost angrily. "Of course I want you! Nobody knows better than I do that Loriol and I don't stand an earthly of winning. She's good, but not that good. She hasn't had enough experience. But she's dead keen, and—well, I don't really mind forfeiting my chances of winning, to please her, and if—if you'll be sensible about it. Sam's a good sort, he'll be no end bucked to have you. I shouldn't be a bit surprised if you won."

Peta's quick temper flared. He was talking to her as if she were a child who only needed to be bribed with a piece of candy!

She said furiously, "Do you think I'd care whether we won or not? And do you mind telling me since when Sam Merridew has been a 'good sort'? Last season you didn't have a good word to say for him, you called him a rotten sport and a bit of a bounder! Now, when it suits you, it seems you're prepared to shuffle me off to him and blow the consequences!"

"Well, it doesn't have to be Sam. . . ."

"Just so long as you can salve your conscience!" Peta interrupted him with absolute contempt. "Hasn't it ever occurred to you that it's sailing with *you* I care about? That the only reason I was looking forward to next week's regatta was because I knew how much it meant to you? I mean, I thought I knew! You've changed even more than I thought!"

Mike's face was brick-red. "For heaven's sake! Loriol said you'd go off the deep end and it appears she was right! Have it your own way, then, if you feel so badly about it. I'll sail with you, Loriol will just have to watch."

"Oh no, she won't!" Pride had come to Peta's rescue and she was already regretting that she had shown her hurt and disappointment so plainly. "Nothing would induce me to sail with you now!"

"I suppose you think I'm a louse?" Mike asked grimly.

"No. Just an idiot." Peta's voice shook in spite of herself. Now or never. "Mike, I know you're mad about Loriol, but haven't you got the sense to see that she doesn't really care a brass button about you? She—she's just using you for her own ends!"

She hadn't meant to come out with it quite so baldly, and she knew from the expression on Mike's face that she had made him furiously angry.

"An interesting observation, but a little wide of the mark, my dear! You should be a bit more careful before you start making wild accusations of that sort. I'm in love with Loriol, yes, but I've got every reason to believe that she's beginning to feel the same way about me!"

"She isn't! She's—" Peta stopped short. She'd been going to say "She's in love with Nicholas", but if she did Mike would be bound to ask how she knew. And she'd promised Loriol that she wouldn't say a word to anyone. She bit her lip. For a moment she was sorely tempted, but it was only for a moment. She'd never broken a promise yet.

She felt a choking, deep in her throat, and the silence grew. Mike turned and began walking away with an impatient stride.

Peta watched him go. It was the first time they had quarrelled in all their years of friendship and nothing could ever be the same again.

"Hey! What's the matter, my dear? You look as though you'd lost a shilling and found sixpence!"

Stephen's kindly voice sounded at her elbow and she

looked up into his pleasant, ugly face with its humourous mouth and penetrating eyes. She knew from his expression that he realised that she and Mike had been quarrelling and she was acutely conscious of his unspoken sympathy. Come to that, everyone, when they knew about the regatta, would feel sorry for her, and her pride revolted at the thought. Somehow, she told herself grimly, she'd have to make it patently obvious that she couldn't care less!

In the event it was Richard Mayne who made it possible. On her next visit to the hospital he told her that the doctor had said that if he continued to progress at his present rate he would probably be able to return home the following Saturday or Sunday.

"Then I'll fetch you." Peta's offer was spontaneous. It was only afterwards that she remembered the regatta and realised that she had been thrown a life-line.

Richard's face, so much more lined in the last two weeks, lit up.

"That would be good of you, my dear. But a Saturday afternoon? Are you sure there isn't something else you'd rather be doing? You have so little free time, and I've monopolised so much of it lately."

"I wouldn't be doing anything else. I'd like to fetch you."

At least, she thought ruefully, she'd have an answer ready for those who wanted to know why she wasn't at the regatta with Mike. It wouldn't satisfy them, of course, but it might silence them.

She looked at Richard, her brow creasing into an anxious little frown. He oughtn't to go back to that lonely cottage, with only Mrs. Davies to look after him. He needed proper care. But there'd been no reply from Celia Montel to the letter she had sent her, and she was beginning to think there never would be. Perhaps Celia resented her interference, or did not intend to court a possible rebuff.

She said: "I don't like to think of you being alone in that cottage, after you've been so ill."

"It won't be for long. I shan't stay until the end of the summer, as I'd originally planned. I want to finish your portrait, my dear, then I'll be off. I've a hankering for Italy and I've got good friends there."

"I'll miss you."

It was true. She had become very fond of Richard, and talked of him often at Greylings. Even so, her casual announcement of her plans for Saturday did not pass without surprised comment from Ann.

"Saturday?" She looked up, forgetting that she was supposed to be pouring coffee into a cup and slopped most of it into the saucer instead. "But, dear, what about the regatta? I thought you and Mike were so keen to win that trophy for the third year running? You said it had never been done before."

Peta answered her lightly. "Well, Mike's still got a good chance. I'm not indispensable."

"But who is going to crew for him, if you're not?" Ann looked perplexed. She never realised what was going on, even if it was right under her nose.

Loriol leant forward, her smile as bland as cream.

"I'm substituting for Peta, Miss Devlin. Actually I'm rather thrilled to have the chance, it all sounds as though it's going to be terribly exciting."

She looked at Nicholas, whose brown face had remained completely impassive.

"I hope you'll come to cheer us on, Nicholas? Your moral support would be welcome."

To Peta, it sounded almost like a challenge. She found herself holding her breath, but Nicholas merely inclined his head.

"You'll survive without it. What is it they say?— Fortune favours the bold." His lips smiled, but his eyes did not. He turned to Peta.

"Perhaps you'd like me to come with you to the hospital on Saturday, Peta? Mr. Mayne may be a little more comfortable in my car than in yours: it's bigger."

There was a momentary silence, broken by a clatter as Loriol's spoon fell to the floor. Then Peta said quietly, "Thank you, Nicholas. I'm sure you'd be a great help."

Later, helping Ann to wash up, she realised that the elder woman was disturbed by the tensions and undercurrents which she sensed but could not comprehend.

"Isn't Mike upset because you won't be sailing with him on Saturday? You two have always done things together."

"Then it's time we both had a change."

I'm learning, Peta thought bitterly, marvelling at her own nonchalance.

Ann shot her a swift, uneasy glance. "Well, if you both feel like that, then of course . . . Dr. Waring didn't sound too happy about Miss Kent, though, did he?"

Peta, carefully polishing a glass until it glittered, did not answer immediately.

"No, he didn't."

Ann lowered her voice confidentially. "I've sometimes thought . . . well, Miss Kent has dropped one or two hints . . . that there's something between those two. Mind you, it may not come to anything. I rather hope it doesn't."

"Why do you say that?"

"Oh, I don't know. I don't think I like Miss Kent as much as I did at first. She's very beautiful, of course, and she can be quite charming. But she's got a hard centre. I don't think she's right for Dr. Waring."

She caught sight of Peta's astonished expression and gave an embarrassed little laugh.

"Listen to me! I've got no right to express an opinion, it's none of my business. But I like Dr. Waring and I'd be sorry if he made a mistake."

That, from Ann, was amazing. Evidently she, at any rate, was shrewd enough to see through Loriol's airs and graces, Peta thought. It was odd that Nicholas wasn't, except that it was probably difficult for any man to be completely objective when a woman appealed so blatantly to the senses as did Loriol Kent. Nevertheless, it seemed that he wasn't going to allow himself to be stampeded into the proposal she wanted so badly, nor did he have any intention of acting the part of the jealous lover. In that case, it surely couldn't be long before Loriol realised that she was making a big mistake?

She couldn't help wondering why it was that Nicholas

had offered to accompany her to the hospital. Was it sheer kind-heartedness, or had he intended it as a kind of retaliation? She couldn't quite make up her mind, though Loriol made it quite clear what she thought. On the day of the regatta she stopped Peta on the stairs and there was more than a hint of malice in her green eyes as she said, "Tit for tat, Peta, but don't forget there is a difference. Mike really *wants* to be with me!"

Peta brushed past her without replying. Loriol had already indicated that although she didn't like Nicholas to pay attention to anyone except herself, she didn't really count her, Peta, as opposition. Nevertheless the barbed words rankled, and when on Saturday afternoon she came out of the house to find Nicholas already in his car, waiting for her, she half wished that she could tell him that she had decided to go alone after all.

Then he smiled, the extraordinarily attractive smile that made him look so much younger, and she decided she was being silly. Nicholas wasn't like Loriol, he didn't use people like pawns!

He held open the door for her to get in and said lightly, "Everything ready for the great homecoming?"

"Yes. I didn't have to go to work today, so I spent the morning at the cottage."

She slipped into the front passenger seat and sat there rather shyly, her hands clasped tightly in her lap. The car glided forward, and for a while Nicholas drove without speaking.

Then he shot her a swift, searching glance and said, "What's up, Peta? Not ructions again, I hope?"

She knew what he meant and a small reluctant smile tugged at her lips.

"Not since you've been back. You know, Nicholas, I never knew until you went away how much I owed to you, and how often you kept the peace."

He laughed. "I've had plenty of practice. I've got to know the Professor pretty well during the past two years."

"You certainly know how to handle him. He's been like a lamb just lately, but the book's going well again, isn't it? I heard him reading the latest chapter to Ann last night. I didn't understand it all, but parts were quite interesting."

His lips quirked. "I'm glad you bothered to listen. I thought you found archaeology a dead bore?"

"Well, I used to, but . . ." She stopped, embarrassed. She could hardly tell him that it was he who had suddenly made her realise that there was more to archaeology than dust and dry bones and ruined buildings. He could make the study of the ancient world sound like an exciting adventure, and he had the gift of infecting other people with his own enthusiasm.

She said slowly, "I suppose I was blinded by prejudice. It was rather silly of me."

He did not reply, but she saw the smile deepen. He was driving fast: the car was eating up the miles. She thought how odd it was that she was here, sitting quite contentedly beside Nicholas, when she ought to have been skimming over the water in *Romany*, with Mike as her faithful companion. Why didn't she feel utterly wretched? She frowned to herself. She *did* mind . . . of course she minded! It was just that she was being sensible and making the best of a bad job.

In some ways she was surprised at herself for feeling so light-hearted, but she put it down to the fact that she was pleased that Richard was coming home—at last.

He was waiting for them at the hospital, having already said goodbye to the doctors and nurses who had taken care of him throughout his illness. He was looking quite well, Peta thought, and he seemed delighted that Nicholas had come along too.

He sat next to Nicholas on the way home and Peta, sitting in the back and listening to their conversation, realised with satisfaction that they were already firm friends. Perhaps, if Nicholas had any free time, he would drop in to see Richard occasionally. It would do the elder man the world of good.

At any rate the cottage was looking welcoming . . . almost homelike. The sun was streaming through the studio window, she had filled every vase she could find with gay summer flowers, and a small table was already laid for tea. Ann had made feather-light scones and her special fruit cake, and had also contributed a jar of honey and a pot of her homemade strawberry jam.

"What a feast!" Richard said, smiling as he lowered himself into a shabby but comfortable easy chair. "You'll both stay and have tea with me, won't you?"

Peta looked at Nicholas.

"Of course," he said promptly. "I was hoping I was going to be asked."

"I laid the table for three. If you'll excuse me I'll go and put the kettle on," said Peta, and went into the tiny kitchen.

Richard's gaze followed her.

"I wonder what's wrong with that child? Something's happened to her in the last few weeks. She's changed. Except when she remembers to make herself smile she's much too serious. She's lost that carefree, gamine look she used to have."

"Yes, she has." Nicholas did not hint at his fuller knowledge.

Richard sighed. "I suppose she had to grow up some time, but I'm sorry. She was an enchanting child. What is it? Trouble with that young Viking of hers? I've noticed she hasn't mentioned him lately."

"Young Viking?" For a moment Nicholas looked blank, then he gave a wry smile. "Is that what you call him? Yes, I suppose it's apt."

"I had the impression that those two were soul-mates." Richard was still frowning. "I wonder what upset the apple-cart?"

"What apple-cart?" said a clear young voice, and Peta came into the room bearing a milk jug and a big china teapot, liberally patterned with huge cabbage roses.

"Heavens!" Nicholas exclaimed, springing up to take them from her and avoiding her question. "How many cups apiece does that hold, Peta? You wouldn't need a tea urn with that around!"

"I think there's a smaller one somewhere," Richard

said vaguely. "Where did you find that monstrosity, Peta? I'd no idea I was harbouring such relics!"

"On a shelf in the pantry. The small one you're referring to has no lid and the spout is cracked!" Peta retorted.

Nicholas was laughing. "Peta, you disappoint me! You're the last person I'd have thought would worry over a cracked spout!"

"I mightn't, if you were going to do the pouring!" Peta said cheerfully. "Mr. Mayne, do have one of Ann's scones. They're delicious."

"I can corroborate that. Miss Devlin's cooking is the only reason I've remained so long at Greylings."

Nicholas spoke lightly, but Peta was conscious of an odd little chill. In spite of herself she couldn't help thinking of the real reason, and for a moment it almost seemed as if the shadow of Loriol was standing at her elbow.

It was the only discordant moment. Tea was a cheerful meal, with everyone, even Richard, talking and laughing a lot. Afterwards Nicholas insisted on helping Peta to wash up, claiming that he was an expert with a tea towel.

Peta, cheeks flushed, a voluminous apron belonging to Mrs. Davies tied round her slim waist, was carefully stacking the china when there was a knock at the door. Nicholas answered it, to disclose Mrs. Davies on the threshold, fat and beaming.

"I just thought I'd look in to say 'Welcome home' to Mr. Mayne," she explained. "I'll be in tomorrow, same as usual, but I thought maybe there was something I could do for him tonight."

She caught sight of Peta standing by the sink and surprise quivered across her plump, heavy-jowled face.

"Gracious, miss, I didn't expect to see you here! I thought for sure you'd be at the regatta!"

Mrs. Davies' son worked at a local boatyard and she was well informed about all river events.

"Oh, I decided to give it the go-by this year," Peta said lightly.

She might have known that Mrs. Davies wouldn't be content to leave it at that.

"What about Mike Mandeville?" she demanded. "Is he sailing?" Then, as Peta nodded. "Well, I never! Got his new girl-friend with him, has he? Never you mind, miss, there's as good fish in the sea as ever came out, if the saying's to be believed!"

Her small beady eyes, bright with curiosity and interest, darted from Peta to Nicholas, whom she had never seen before. A good-natured soul on the whole, her one big failing was her insatiable interest in other people's affairs. She had felt sorry for Peta when she had heard, via the village grapevine, that Mike Mandeville had taken up with somebody else, but judging from appearances Peta was by no means inconsolable. The speculative expression on her face was very plain to read, and Peta felt acutely embarrassed.

It was Nicholas who made a brief and non-committal reply to Mrs. Davies and Nicholas, polite but determined, who finally ushered her out.

When he came back Peta attempted to laugh. "That's the worst of living in a village! Everything gets gossiped about!"

She looked up at him and her heart gave a sudden jolt. His face was so hard and angry. Did he care so much then, what people thought and said about Mike and Loriol?

"When I meet people like Mrs. Davies I begin to see the virtues of the old-time ducking stool!" he said grimly.

"Oh, she means well——" Peta began, but just at that moment Richard called her and she hurried into the studio to see what he wanted.

He was standing in front of his easel, looking down at the half-finished portrait which, previously, had been standing with its face to the wall.

"My dear, can you give me just one more sitting?" he asked. "I won't need any more. I must apologise for my tardiness, but that's what comes of being old and feeble."

Nicholas had followed Peta into the studio and now she heard his startled exclamation.

"You didn't tell me that Mr. Mayne was painting your portrait!"

She flushed scarlet and began to stammer something incoherently, but Richard cut her short. His quick, sudden smile touched his thin lips.

"Peta thinks I'm wasting my time. I believe it's one of the best things I've ever done. What do you say, Waring?"

Nicholas was standing very still in front of the canvas. His back was towards Peta and so she could not see his expression, but there was an odd note in his voice as he said slowly, "I agree with you, sir. It's a wonderful likeness."

"You haven't seen the landscapes." Anxious to distract Nicholas's attention from the portrait, Peta spoke breathlessly. "May I show him, please, Mr. Mayne? Look! This one is my favourite. And isn't this lovely? It's Thurne Mill, of course."

Nicholas showed proper enthusiasm, but it seemed to Peta that he was a little distrait. Perhaps, she thought, he wanted to get back to Greylings so that he was there when Loriol came home. They ought to be going now, anyway: Richard ought to rest for a while. He was beginning to look very tired.

Yet, when they finally did take their departure, she was conscious once more of that queer undefined little ache in her heart. Richard, watching them walk to the car, noticed the slight droop to her slender shoulders and sudden anger blazed within him. He'd give a good deal to make that child happy again, he thought, and then sighed. He didn't even know what was wrong and if he did, there was nothing he could do. He couldn't even manage his own life, he reflected bitterly, let alone somebody else's!

CHAPTER NINE

IT was from Holly, whom she met in the village, that Peta suddenly learnt how Mike and Loriol had fared at the regatta.

"We all had to go and watch," Holly told her gloomily. "I didn't want to, I kicked up an awful fuss, but Mum made me." Her face brightened. "It was an awful flop, I can tell you that. Mike and Loriol didn't come anywhere. She's useless in a boat, really, even though Mike does keep on saying how well she's getting on."

"Do you think that's fair? She strikes me as the kind of person who does most things well," Peta said quietly.

Holly looked at her in genuine admiration. "I think you're being a brick about all this, Peta! If I were you I'd want to strangle Loriol Kent! Did—did you mind frightfully, not taking part in the regatta?"

"I did mind, just at first, but then I had something else to do and I forgot all about it. Or almost."

"Oh yes, you and Dr. Waring fetched that artist man from hospital, didn't you? He's nice, isn't he?"

"Who?" Peta asked, laughing. "The artist man or Dr. Waring?"

"I don't know the artist man. I'm sure he's nice, but I really meant Dr. Waring. He's got a terrific sense of humour, I just love the way his eyes crinkle up at the corners when he laughs." Her brow furrowed. "You know, I simply can't think why Loriol bothers about Mike when she's got a dish like that right under her nose! You'd think she wouldn't have eyes for anyone else, wouldn't you—except that perhaps he's got a bit more sense than my idiot brother has! Or else she's trying to make him jealous. You know what they say— all's fair in love and war!"

"You've got a fertile imagination, Holly Mandeville!"

Holly giggled. "I have, haven't I? I may be a novelist when I grow up. I can think of some super plots and my English mistress says that my essays show promise. But I might take up archaeology instead. Dr. Waring makes it sound fascinating."

Peta raised her brows and Holly laughed.

"Oh, didn't you know that I went for a walk with him the other day? I took him right over the marshes. We're quite good friends now, he told me lots of frightfully interesting things. We talked about you, too," she added mischievously.

"Me?" Peta stared at her, alarm written across her face. "Holly, what did you say?"

Holly's eyes were wide and innocent. "Oh, nothing very much. I just said I liked you better than any other girl I knew and—and that I wished you were my sister. I *do* wish that, you know, Peta."

"You and Dickon have always treated me like one. That needn't necessarily change," Peta said quietly.

"We've always thought of you as one of the family. Mum has, too." Holly saw Peta's expression change and added, a little uncomfortably, "Oh, I know she makes a great fuss of Loriol, but that's only because she thinks she's waking Mike up a bit. She—she's still very fond of you. It's her birthday on Friday, you know, and she's going to hold a sort of impromptu party. She's going to invite you and Loriol and Dr. Waring and Joan and Roger Talbot and—oh, tons of other people! It will be a fearful squash, I expect, but that won't matter. You *will* come, won't you, Peta? I'll hate it if you aren't there."

She might have added, but didn't, that she had already told her mother that she would stay in her room unless Peta was invited. She was convinced that the elder girl was bravely nursing a broken heart and her romantic imagination was busily fashioning a secret drama out of the situation. She was also young enough to believe that, in the end, true love conquered all.

Peta looked at her, dismayed. After her quarrel with Mike—oh no, she couldn't!

Holly brushed aside her protest. "It will look jolly queer if you refuse! You keep trying to pretend you don't care about Mike and Loriol, but if you stay away everyone will think it's because of them!"

Peta bit her lip. There was a lot of truth in what Holly had said. On the other hand, if she went it was bound to be a very uncomfortable evening.

In spite of herself her thoughts flew back to Mrs. Mandeville's last birthday. She always organised some kind of special celebration, and last year it had been a visit to the theatre. She and Mike had sat together, laughed together and afterwards it was Mike who had taken her home. This year. . . . She sighed. This year things were very different!

Margaret's invitation—a charmingly worded little note—came the next day. Peta thought about it all morning and eventually decided, more as a gesture of bravado than anything else, to accept. The only problem was what she could wear. She'd never worried before, but somehow for this one occasion it seemed absolutely vital that she should look reasonably presentable. Not, of course, that she could ever hope to vie with Loriol!

In the end she sought Marjorie's advice. Ann knew even less about clothes than Peta did, and although Marjorie never aimed at elegance, whatever she wore always looked "right".

"Where do I buy my clothes?" Marjorie sounded surprised. "Norwich, usually, but no particular shop. Why Peta?"

Peta told her, and Marjorie looked thoughtful. "When is the 'do', did you say? Friday? Heavens, you haven't got much time!" She was silent for a moment or two and then she smiled. "I've got an idea. I want to do some shopping myself: I shall need some maternity clothes soon and I'm dying to make a start on the baby's layette. Suppose we both play truant on Friday and go on a shopping spree? You can help me to choose some things for the baby and I'll help you to choose a dress. Don't you think that would be rather fun?"

Peta's eyes had begun to sparkle. "It would be marvellous! But—Friday? We can't both play truant, can we? How would your husband manage on his own?"

"No problem," Marjorie said cheerfully. "My brother-in-law is coming to stay with us for a few days: he'll be here on Thursday. He's ex-R.N. and mad keen on sailing, he'll simply love to help Stephen out. The two of them should be able to cope quite easily, we needn't worry a bit!"

"It would be marvellous," Peta repeated, and Marjorie laughed.

"Then that's settled! We'll find you a gorgeous dress, Peta, with a figure like yours you're a couturier's dream!"

At dinner that night it was Loriol who brought up the subject of Margaret's invitation.

"Of course you'll be accepting, won't you, Peta?" she asked sweetly. "Dickon and Holly seem to be *so* fond of you and I know you wouldn't disappoint them."

The congé was unmistakable, but Peta met her gaze squarely.

"No, I wouldn't."

"And you, Nicholas?" Loriol's voice became coaxing. "I hope *you* are coming. There'll be dancing, I expect, and it seems a long, long time since we used to dance the night away! Do you remember Lima, and the night we went to the masquerade?" Her long golden lashes veiled her eyes and her smile was soft and languorous, as though she was recalling a rainbowed memory.

Peta's heart missed a beat. These were old tactics . . . evidently it was back to Square One! She wondered what impression, if any, was being made. Nicholas was certainly smiling back, but there was something in his smile . . .

All he said, however, as he rose to his feet was, "Distance lends enchantment, my dear. But yes, I'll be accepting Mrs. Mandeville's invitation. In fact, I wouldn't miss her party for the world."

Peta couldn't help feeling rather puzzled. Ann had mentioned, earlier on, that Nicholas had told her he wasn't going. What had made him change his mind? She had the oddest conviction that he'd done so on the spur of the moment, in which case it must have been

Loriol's persuasion that had done the trick. That play with her eyelashes was very effective!

She found herself wondering just what it was that had happened on the night of the masquerade to make it so memorable, and pulled herself up sharply. It was absolutely nothing to do with her.

Driven by the feeling of restlessness which was becoming so familiar, she decided to go and see Richard. It was a cold and blustery evening, and as she walked quickly along the lane the wind tugged furiously at her hair and skirt and sent the dark clouds scurrying across the sky. Someone had lit a bonfire, and with every puff of wind came the good smell of woodsmoke. With a sense of shock she realised that summer was drawing to a close. Autumn would soon be upon them, bringing—what?

"I'm getting morbid," she told herself, and tried to reason herself into a happier frame of mind. If anyone needed a cheerful companion it was surely poor Richard.

When she reached the cottage she was surprised to see a small grey saloon standing outside. Had Richard already got a visitor? For a moment she hesitated, wondering if she should turn back there and then, but decided to knock and see. If necessary she could always beat a hasty retreat.

She tapped at the door, and as she did so became conscious of the rise and fall of voices within. He *had* got a visitor, she thought, but before she had time to wonder who it could be Richard's voice called "Come in."

Gently she turned the handle of the door. She put in her head, but her greeting died on her lips and she stood stockstill from sheer surprise. Richard was sitting in his favourite easy chair, but a fair-haired girl was sitting on the shabby rug at his feet, one slim brown arm flung across his knee. She looked up at Peta and smiled, then jumped to her feet and came forward with her hand outstretched.

"Peta! It *is* Peta, isn't it? Father said he was sure

135

you'd drop in this evening, though I would have come to see you if you hadn't."

The girl in the photograph! Celia Montel! Richard's estranged daughter! Dazed and incredulous, she looked from her to the artist. There was an unmistakable resemblance between the two faces, but what struck her most forcibly was the change in Richard's. He looked years younger, and happier than she would ever have believed possible.

He said, laughing, "Yes, Peta, it's Celia. Don't pretend you don't know what's brought her here, you minx: I've already seen the letter you wrote to her and I'm not angry. How could I be, in view of the result?"

"We're both more than grateful—me especially." Celia's radiant smile lit up her whole face. "Father wouldn't answer my original letter because he had some crazy, ridiculous notion that I'd think it was only because he was ill and needed love and attention.—Yes, you do, darling, and Louis and I and the children are going to see that you get it!" she added firmly as Richard protested. "I'd more or less made up my mind that he hadn't forgiven me for—for past misunderstandings, and it wasn't until I read your letter that I realised the true position."

Peta found her tongue at last. "I'd begun to think that I'd made an awful mistake!"

. "Because I didn't reply, you mean? I'm sorry about that, but we were away from home and I didn't have any mail sent on. I found your letter waiting for me when I got back yesterday and I booked a flight straight away. I wasn't sure, in view of the time lapse, whether Father would be here or still in hospital, but I thought that as you'd had the foresight to give me his address I'd try here first.

Peta's eyes were shining. "And it's really all right now? You've forgiven each other?"

"All forgiven and forgotten," Richard said, smiling at them both. "As soon as Celia walked through that door I knew what a silly, obstinate old fool I'd been all these years and how much, in my heart, I'd wanted her back."

Over coffee, which she helped Celia to prepare, Peta heard that Celia had already been trying to persuade her father to make his home with her.

"My husband's firm is sending him to open up a new branch in Switzerland, and we've just bought rather a gorgeous house on Lake Lucerne," she told Peta. "Miles too big for a family of four, really, and it would be just marvellous to have Father living with us."

She looked at Richard. "You know how you've always loved the mountains! Even if you feel that your skiing days are over at least you can enjoy yourself painting the Alpine scenery! And the air will do you the world of good, won't it, Peta?"

Richard's eyes were twinkling. "Same old Celia, same old enthusiasms! You tempt me, my dear, but suppose we wait a while before we make any dramatic decisions? I'd like to get to know my son-in-law and my grandchildren, though, so I think that a protracted holiday would be quite in order."

"Louis is a darling. I always told you he was!"

A shadow passed over Richard's face and, seeing it, Celia rushed quickly on. "The boys are little fiends, but quite nice little fiends, for all that. Matthew—he's the elder—is very much like you, Father. He's never happier than when he's daubing paint all over the place, though I admit that usually most of it ends up bespattering his person! You'll have a willing pupil if you want one!"

Peta, sitting with her chin cupped in her hands, thought how wonderful it was to hear Richard laughing like that. He was revelling in his daughter's company as in sunshine after rain: he must have missed her even more than she had suspected.

When at last she rose to go Celia accompanied her to the door. Her merry face suddenly sober, she said quietly, "I really can't thank you enough for that letter, Peta. Knowing Father as well as you do, it must have taken real courage to write it. I love him, but he can be quite terrifying when he's angry!"

"He has never been anything but kindness itself to me."

"He's changed a lot. Mellowed." She was silent for a moment. "I don't suppose he told you what caused the rift between us, but it was mostly my fault. I fell head over heels in love with Louis when I was barely eighteen, and we wanted to get married right away. Father was terribly upset because, apart from the fact that he thought we were too young, he believed that I had a talent for painting and that I oughtn't to let it go to waste. He offered me R.A.D.A., the Slade, anything and everything except what I really wanted. In the end I—I ran away, and Louis and I were married in Paris. The day after our wedding Father wrote to say that as I had so completely disregarded his wishes he never wanted to see me again."

"How awful for both of you!"

"Yes. It's been the one thing that has prevented my being completely happy. I've missed him terribly. Do you think I'll be able to persuade him to come and live with us in Switzerland?"

"I don't think you'll have a great deal of difficulty, once he gets used to the idea." Peta said, smiling.

"I want you to come and stay with us, too. Father's terribly fond of you, you know." Celia's voice was warm and she laid her hand on Peta's arm. "I'd like to know you better, but I've got to go back tomorrow, I'm afraid; this was only meant to be a flying visit. I haven't got a nanny just at present, and I've had to leave the babes with Louis. He can stand the strain for a limited period, but it has to be strictly limited, bless him!"

"I saw the children's photograph. I thought they looked angelic!" Peta protested.

"Appearances are deceptive! Wait until you've made their acquaintance, you'll soon change your tune!" Celia said darkly. She gave Peta's arm a friendly squeeze. "I really meant that invitation, you know. Father says that you think there's nowhere like Norfolk, but I believe you'd adore Switzerland. Think about it, won't you? I'd simply love you to come."

She's nice, really nice, Peta thought as she began walking back to Greylings. Whatever the old scores,

Richard Mayne was fortunate in his daughter. He need never be lonely again.

The wind had died down a little and the moon was nearly full in a clear sky. As she turned into Greylings' driveway a tall figure loomed up beside her and she realised it was Nicholas. Her heart seemed to turn over, but it was, of course, only that he had startled her.

"Hello. Isn't it a lovely night?" she said breathlessly.

"Beautiful. Just right for nocturnal prowling."

At least Loriol wasn't with him. Involuntarily Peta glanced towards the house. There was a light on in the library, so probably Loriol and the Professor were both working. That explained it.

"Have you been to see Richard Mayne? I meant to go myself today, but didn't have time. Perhaps tomorrow."

"You'll find him a different person. Something marvellous has happened." Without disclosing the role that she herself had played, Peta told him about Celia's surprise appearance.

"Loriol told me she was at school with his daughter. So she's turned up, has she? What is she like?" Nicholas asked.

"Delightful."

"I'm glad about that." Nicholas paused to throw away a half-smoked cigarette. The light from the pale, moon-washed sky shone on to his face, and Peta suddenly realised how tired he was looking. Tired, and a little drawn. Obeying an odd impulse she asked, "Have you made up your mind about Peru yet?"

"Peru? Oh yes, I think so. Frankly, I think it was mere foolishness that I didn't give my answer on the spot." He gave a short, rather hard laugh. "Have you ever been a victim of delusions, Peta? Delusions or dreams, whatever you like to call them. Perhaps they amount to the same thing."

What on earth did he mean? Was he referring to Loriol? She looked at him, bewildered, and he put a hand under her chin and turned her face up to his. For a long moment he looked intently into her eyes.

"Suppose you tell me what would be your dream-come-true, Peta? I'd be interested to know."

She wanted to answer, but couldn't. The turmoil of feeling aroused in her by his touch almost staggered her. She stood quite still, trembling a little, and she saw his expression change, heard him take a quick breath. Then there came a sudden rush of wings, and a flock of wild geese passed overhead, darkening the sky and filling the air with the rushing of their passage. The spell was broken. She jerked herself away and began walking quickly towards the house. Over her shoulder she said with a laugh. "You once told me to grow up, Nicholas. It's only children who believe that dreams sometimes come true."

It was the kind of remark that the old Peta would never have made. She herself knew that she had changed. Sometimes, when she thought of the portrait that Richard had started only a few weeks ago, she had a feeling that there was little resemblance between that happy, carefree girl and the shadowy-eyed stranger whom she now saw reflected in her bedroom mirror.

Richard had at last finished the portrait. He had put the final touches to it just after Celia had left him to drive back to London in her hired car, for she was due to catch an afternoon plane from Heathrow Airport. Neither had enjoyed the parting, but both were comforted by the knowledge that it was only for a short time.

When Peta called to see him that evening she found him brimming with new enthusiasm and vitality, and this time it was she who almost envied him his high spirits. He greeted her warmly, his affection for her deepened by his realisation that it was to her he owed his present happiness.

He was full of his plans for the future, and they had been chatting for some time before he suddenly said, "By the way, Waring and the girl you've occasionally mentioned—Loriol Kent—came to see me this afternoon."

Peta stared at him, her face suddenly stricken. Nicholas had brought Loriol *here*? Why? What right had he to do that? Loriol didn't care about Richard, she wouldn't have lifted her little finger to help him!

She was appalled to find herself shaken by such a storm of jealousy that for a moment she could not speak, though luckily Richard seemed to notice nothing amiss.

"I'd told Celia how it was that you'd come to find out that I had a daughter. She said that she vaguely remembered Loriol Kent as a skinny child with pigtails and a brace round her teeth, so I imagine she would have had a bit of difficulty in recognising the grown-up version! She certainly is a gorgeous creature, isn't she?"

Richard was an artist, and it was with an artist's appreciation that he spoke.

Through stiff lips Peta said, "Yes. You should have painted her, not me. I told you there were lots of girls far prettier!"

Something in her voice caught Richard's attention. He looked at her sharply, and the bleakness of her expression stabbed at his heart. For the first time hints dropped by Mrs. Davies—hints he had largely ignored—seemed to make some kind of sense. Could Loriol Kent possibly be the beautiful blonde, who, according to Mrs. Davies, had captivated Peta's young Viking?

Mentally cursing himself for a tactless fool, he said quickly, "Even if I had seen Loriol Kent long before I met you I should never have felt the slightest desire to paint her. She is beautiful, yes, but it is a superficial beauty. I have painted dozens of women like her in my time. But *you*, Peta. . . ." He stopped short, then came towards her and took her face in his hands in much the same way as Nicholas had done the night before.

Very gently he said, "You once asked me why I wanted to paint you, Peta, and I wouldn't tell you. I'd like to tell you now. I saw in you, my dear, an enchanting and unusual child and I saw, also, a glimpse of the beautiful and lovable woman you would become."

He saw her eyes widen incredulously and smiled a little sadly. "You've begun to grow up already. There'll be a day, quite soon, when you'll look into the mirror and know that what I've told you is no more than the truth."

She didn't really believe him, he was just being kind, and yet somehow his words eased her sore heart. They made it possible, the following day, for her to show an enthusiasm for the shopping expedition which might otherwise have been missing, for she had begun to think that she was being foolish and that it wouldn't matter what she wore at Margaret's party. Probably she could turn up in sackcloth and ashes and no one would even notice!

Marjorie was frankly determined to make the most of what was as much of a holiday for her as it was for Peta. She bought two very pretty maternity outfits— "I'm lucky, I haven't really begun to show yet, but my clothes are becoming awfully tight around the waist!" she said, laughing—and then she and Peta spent a blissful hour choosing tiny, frilly garments for the expected arrival. Marjorie was sure that it would be a girl, and insisted on referring to her as 'Annabel'.

"Aren't these gorgeous? I'll have three, I think," she said, picking up an exquisite pillowcase and exclaiming delightedly over the delicate embroidery.

Suddenly the thought of a baby's sleeping, downy head on the lace-trimmed pillowcase, long lashes curving on rose-petal cheeks, stirred Peta with a feeling that was half pain, half delight. Anxious to dispel such traitorous feelings she said hurriedly, "What about those blankets? They look beautifully warm. And may I buy Annabel's shawl, please? I'd like her to have a present from me."

Marjorie's blue eyes laughed at her over the pile of purchases.

"You may with pleasure, but in return I want you to accept a gift from me. After we've chosen your dress I'm going to take you to a hairdresser's and then to a beautician's! Yes, I mean it!" as Peta gave a horrified exclamation. "You're a woman now, not a schoolgirl, and unfortunately a woman's world is an entirely competitive one! You may as well make the most of whatever weapons there are to hand!"

Remorselessly she swept Peta off to make the most important purchase of the day. Left to herself Peta would probably have bought the first garment which was a pretty colour and which fitted, but Marjorie was far harder to please. She vetoed dress after dress, and then, just as Peta was beginning to think that there really couldn't be many shops left, they saw it. The perfect dress, shimmering, soft and silky, on a rail with several others in a small boutique.

Marjorie did not even hesitate. "Try it on!" she commanded, and when Peta complied she gave a sigh of utter satisfaction. No colour could have better suited Peta's chestnut hair and hazel-brown eyes than the soft amber of that dress and it looked just right on her slender body, with its youthful curves.

Marjorie, accustomed as she was to another Peta, a long-legged, blue-denimed tomboy climbing in and out of boats, careless and dishevelled, a creature of rivers and woods and winds, was enraptured.

"Peta, it's beautiful! I don't care how much it costs, that's the one you've got to have!"

Flushed and excited, Peta meekly paid over what she secretly considered an exorbitant sum and was then whirled off to the hairdresser's. A charming young assistant sympathised with her reluctance to have her hair cut (not that she herself would have minded, it just happened to be the only thing on which Ann felt strongly) and showed her how to sweep it up in a simple but elegant style. A visit to a beautician followed and after an instructive half-hour Peta left the shop with an expensive little package which contained everything she needed for her own home use.

Marjorie glanced at her watch. "Well, after all that I simply must have a cup of tea! We've just got time, I think, if we hurry."

They made their way to the large departmental store at which Marjorie had made most of her purchases and took a lift to the restaurant, which was on the top floor.

Marjorie collapsed on to a chair with a sigh of relief and ordered tea cakes.

"I adore shopping, but isn't it exhausting? I shall sleep like a log tonight!"

"You haven't overdone it, have you?" Peta enquired,

glancing at her anxiously and thinking that she looked rather pale under her tan.

"Heavens, no! I've enjoyed every minute! Haven't you?"

"Yes." Peta turned to look at the two packages, one large and one small, lying on the chair beside her and her eyes glowed. Perhaps, she thought hopefully, they would all see tonight that she wasn't a child any longer. Perhaps . . . perhaps she would even succeed in looking attractive, wearing that lovely dress and her new and very becoming make-up!

As if reading her thoughts Marjorie said hesitantly, "Peta, forgive me for saying this, but I can't help realising that you haven't been too happy lately. There's something wrong between you and Mike, isn't there?"

Peta felt the colour rush into her cheeks. "I suppose you've heard all the village gossip!" she said rather bitterly.

"Well . . . you know how things get talked about in a small community. Nobody really means any harm." She paused and stirred up her tea. "I gather Mike's fallen pretty heavily for your guardian's secretary?"

"Yes."

Marjorie frowned. "She's very beautiful, of course, but miles too old for Mike, surely?"

"That aspect doesn't seem to bother him. You've seen her, then?"

"She and Mike were at the Fisherman's Rest the other night when Stephen and I called in for a drink. You know it, I expect—that pretty riverside inn that's just been renovated. It attracts quite a crowd of young people."

Peta gave a mirthless laugh. "Well then, if you've seen Loriol you're probably wondering why on earth I'm worrying about how *I* look tonight!"

Marjorie put down her teacup with such force that the saucer rattled. "Don't be such a goose, Peta! That defeatist attitude isn't a bit like you! Why in heaven's name don't you put up a fight? You're an extremely attractive girl, even if up to now Mike hasn't quite realised it! *Make* him notice you tonight, Peta! You've so much on your side, you know. Old ties count for a lot, and in any case he's probably suffering from a temporary infatuation. Get him back! You can if you try!"

"But . . ." Peta stopped, biting her lip. How could she possibly make Marjorie understand that she didn't even know if she wanted Mike back—at least, not in the way *she* meant! What she wanted she could never have, not even if she fought and won. She and Mike could never return to their old friendly footing: those days were over for good.

Just at that moment Marjorie realised that they had lingered longer over tea than she had intended. "Heavens, Peta, it's gone half-past five. We shall have to fly or you're going to have a job to be ready in time. Shall we get started?"

She drove home as fast as she dared, but nevertheless it was late when she dropped Peta off at her gate. It was also raining fast. Peta groaned and took the extraordinary precaution of tying a headscarf round her hair before making a wild dash for the house. She had only about half an hour in which to get ready, and though normally she could bath and change in ten minutes flat, she was sure that it would take her a lot longer than that tonight.

She flung her damp coat and scarf over the banisters—Ann would hang them up for her later!—and flew up the stairs, taking them two at a time. Ann, coming out into the hall from the kitchen, caught just a glimpse of her flying figure and sighed and then laughed. She too had noticed the change in Peta, but at times like this she wondered whether she would ever be anything but a wild harum-scarum.

She was in for a big surprise. She was talking to Nicholas and Loriol in the drawing room when, rather more than half an hour later. they saw, through the open doorway, Peta slowly descending those same stairs.

In her lovely amber dress she was as straight and shining as a candle flame, her ruddy hair braided into a gleaming coronal around her head, her lips touched with red, her eyebrows darkened and tiny gold drops—

Marjorie's gift—in her ears. For the first time in her life she was wearing eye-shadow, which had the effect of making her eyes look larger and more luminous.

Loriol, herself a vision of beauty in sophisticated black, almost gasped with astonishment. This couldn't be *Peta*! This was an ugly-duckling-turned-into-a-swan with a vengeance! Peta saw the amazement, disbelief and—yes, even chagrin—written plainly on her face and somehow found the courage to look at Nicholas. If there was even a hint of amusement in his grey eyes. . . . !

But there was none. He was standing very still, but though his face gave nothing away his smile was warm as he said lightly, "You look like a daffodil, my dear . . . a daffodil blooming against a winter that has lasted too long." He turned to Ann. "Aren't you proud of your niece, Miss Devlin?"

Ann was almost too stunned to answer. At last she managed to say, "Very . . . you look extremely pretty, dear."

"Quite a transformation," Loriol drawled, and contrived to make it into something rather less than a compliment. She glanced at her watch and added, with a touch of acidity, "A pity that it's taken you quite so long, though. We're going to be frightfully late and I loathe unpunctuality!"

"Oh, not to worry," Nicholas said easily. "Still, let's go. Ready, both of you?"

Loriol swept forward and Peta followed. Then she ran back and gave Ann a swift hug. Half choked with excitement, she felt exactly like Cinderella going to her first ball.

CHAPTER TEN

LORIOL was, in fact, quite right and the party was in full swing when they eventually arrived at Cedar Lodge. There were numerous guests but no apparent crush, since Margaret had exercised her considerable ingenuity in making the most of the space available. She had even decided that, as the rain had now stopped, dancing would be possible on the paved patio which was at the side of the cottage.

Most of the guests knew Peta well, but tonight her appearance with Nicholas and Loriol caused a minor sensation. Loriol, beautiful though she looked, was for once overshadowed, and it was obvious from her expression that the experience was not at all to her liking.

"Peta, my dear! Why, you look quite lovely!" Margaret's astonished but approving greeting was echoed again and again, and though Peta, blushing fiercely, almost wished that the ground would open up and swallow her, Nicholas's continued presence at her side was oddly reassuring. Loriol, it was true, had made several determined efforts to detach him, but he had just as determinedly resisted them.

"He must know how I'm feeling," Peta thought gratefully, and then caught her breath as she saw Mike, an unfamiliar figure in the dinner jacket upon which his mother had insisted, bearing down upon them. It was the first time she had seen him since their quarrel. What was it Marjorie had said? "Get him back . . . you can if you try!"

She moistened her lips a little and smiled nervously. Mike's gaze rested upon her for just a moment, and she saw surprise flicker in his blue eyes. Then he looked at Loriol and his whole face lit up. It was patently obvious that as from that moment no one else existed.

"Loriol!" he said in a low, vibrant voice, and caught both her hands in his.

Peta felt crushed. Whoever else was impressed by her

new look, it certainly wasn't Mike!

It was at that precise moment that Nicholas turned to her with a smile.

"Shall we circulate?" he asked easily, and cupping her elbow in his hand he piloted her across the crowded room, leaving Loriol with her hands still imprisoned.

Hoist with her own petard, Peta thought with a spurt of wry amusement, and wondered if that quirk at the corner of Nicholas's mouth could possibly mean that he was thinking the same thing. At any rate, he couldn't have made it clearer that so far as this party was concerned he was escorting her and not Loriol. Had he decided, perhaps, to beat the latter at her own game?

And then, extraordinarily, she almost forgot about Mike and Loriol. To her enormous surprise she found that she was enjoying herself. She and Nicholas were caught up in a buzz of conversation, moving from one group to another while Dickon and two of his friends steered dexterously between the little clusters with trays of glasses. Peta, who normally drank nothing stronger than cider, found a drink in a tall glass which looked rather like lemonade but tasted much nicer. She almost asked Nicholas what it was and then decided not to display her ignorance.

Everyone was being incredibly nice to her and Nicholas, especially, was charming and gay and attentive. So much so that she was almost inclined to forgive him for the hurt jealousy she had experienced when she had learned that he had taken Loriol to see Richard . . . almost forgot that it was Loriol who held the key to his heart and that if he was neglecting her tonight it was almost certainly part of a deliberate, carefully-laid plan.

Tit for tat . . . and obviously Loriol did not like it at all. Peta caught a glimpse of her from time to time and realised that her usual vivacity was missing. Mike never left her side, but even he did not seem to be enjoying himself to any great extent. His face was grave to the point of glumness: why? Peta wondered.

It was Holly who shed some light on the matter. Nicholas and Peta had made their way to the buffet and came upon Holly unashamedly tucking into a huge plateful of trifle.

"Peta, you look gorgeous! I've been wanting to tell you that for ages, except that I haven't been able to get anywhere near you! That dress is *super*! Where did you get it? And why don't you always do your hair like that? It suits you frightfully! Don't you think so, Dr. Waring?"

"Oh, definitely frightfully!" said Nicholas, laughing.

Holly pouted. "You needn't make fun of my adverbs! I think they're very expressive!" She waved a casual hand at the buffet. "Aren't you going to have anything to eat? I can thoroughly recommend everything within sight: I've tasted it all!"

Peta looked at the long table, heaped with canapés, crisp pasties bulging with mushroom and chicken and lobster, cocktail sausages on sticks, cheese cubes with pineapple, scallop shells filled with creamed crab, petits fours and delicious gateaux, and grinned, her old gamine grin.

"In that case, Holly my love, I should say it's quite likely that you're going to be frightfully, frightfully sick!"

"Oh well, perhaps not all," Holly admitted. "Enough to make this dress bulge at the seams, though. That's the worst of having a mother who's a marvellous cook. One has to be so tremendously strong-minded!"

Nicholas turned aside to speak to the Vicar's wife and Holly seized her chance. Lowering her voice to a confidential whisper, she asked, "What did Mike say when he saw you? Wasn't he impressed? You've certainly taken the skin off Loriol's nose tonight, Peta, she looks awfully glum for her! She's been snapping poor old Mike's head off for nothing and she won't dance with him, says he crushed her toes the first time and they're not expendable!"

"What aren't?" Nicholas asked, as the Vicar's wife moved on.

"Oh—nothing!" Holly said airily. "Oh, heavens, there's Mum beckoning! I'd better see what she wants!"

"A nice child," Nicholas said, laughing.

Before Peta could answer another tray of drinks was brandished in front of her. She was about to take another glass of the lemonade-like mixture when Nicholas forestalled her.

"I shouldn't if I were you," he murmured. "They're a bit potent, especially if you aren't used to alcohol."

"All right. I'll have a tomato juice instead," Peta decided.

"How pedestrian," a familiar voice drawled, and she looked up to find that they had been joined by Mike and Loriol. The beautiful green eyes were like ice. "Enjoying yourselves?"

It was Nicholas who answered. "Very much indeed, thank you," he said easily, and Peta stole a glance at Mike. It hurt her to see him standing there with that troubled expression in his eyes and set expression of mouth, so obviously at the mercy of the girl he had so eagerly taken up and become obsessed by. The worst of it was that she knew from her own experience that here was a trouble for which no sympathy might be offered. Pity would be as welcome as salt on a sore cut. There was nothing that could be done.

Somebody had put another record on the radiogram, a lovely lilting waltz from an old musical. The french windows were open and on the patio several couples were already dancing.

With a little tinkling laugh Loriol held out her hand to Nicholas. Subconsciously Peta noticed that she was wearing a beaten silver bracelet on her upper arm as if to emphasise its slenderness.

"*Our* tune, Nicholas . . . you remember? We simply must have this one together."

It was impossible for Nicholas to decline without being unpardonably rude. Mike and Peta watched them walk out on to the patio, Loriol slender and fragile in a filmy cloud of black, Nicholas more handsome than ever in his faultlessly cut dinner jacket. They certainly danced beautifully together. No one else could hold a candle to them.

Uncomfortably she realised that she and Mike had

been thrown together. She glanced at his face, and realised from his expression that a new and unwelcome suspicion was growing in his mind.

His hands thrust deep into his pockets, he said, "I suppose Loriol and that chap see quite a lot of each other?"

"Well, they are working on the same project." Peta was surprised to find how even her voice sounded. She looked away. Nicholas and Loriol were dancing very close to each other, almost cheek to cheek. She tried desperately to think of something to say to Mike, but everything that suggested itself seemed stupid. How odd—with Mike, too, to whom once she had poured out everything, certain of sympathy.

"What have you done to yourself?" Mike spoke so abruptly that she almost jumped.

"Done?"

"Yes. I prefer you the way you usually look, not all dolled up like that."

It was on the tip of Peta's tongue to tell him indignantly that he had forfeited the right to criticise her appearance, but she checked the impulse. He looked too unhappy for her to hurt him further.

She thought again about what Marjorie had said and was astonished to find that it had absolutely no relevance to her present feelings. The discovery was shattering. She didn't want to be standing here, with Mike. She wanted. . . . But at the thought of what she wanted a fiery blush spread upwards from her throat and she cast a panic-stricken look at Mike almost as if she suspected him of being a mind-reader.

He was still watching the dancers, his face hard and set. She said in a suffocated voice, "I—I want to powder my nose. Please excuse me," and fled. It was more by luck than by good judgment that she fled in the right direction and presently found herself in Holly's pretty blue-and-white bedroom, which tonight was being used as the guests' powder room. She sank down on to the bed, trembling uncontrollably, but at the sound of voices on the stairs she started up. Oh, she didn't want to talk to anyone now!

Behind the thick blue velvet curtains was a wide window seat. She had sat on it with Holly many times. Swiftly she darted across the room and disappeared behind the curtains just as the bedroom door opened. Pressing her burning cheeks against the cold glass of the window, she tried to control her unsteady breathing.

"I suppose this is Holly's room." That was Loriol's voice. She'd know those distinctive tones anywhere. And the woman with her sounded like Joan Talbot, the wife of the local veterinary surgeon.

What an idiot she'd look if someone decided to draw the curtains, Peta thought. She began to wish that she had not been silly enough to hide, and she wished it more than ever when a few seconds later she realised with a stab of horror that they were talking about her.

"How that Peta child has improved," Joan Talbot was saying. "I hardly recognised her at first. She's quite a little beauty, isn't she?"

"Yes, I suppose she does look quite pretty tonight." Loriol's voice was cool.

"Her escort certainly seems to think so!" Joan Talbot peered into a mirror and pursed her mouth as she applied fresh lipstick.

It was too late to declare herself. Peta, her fingernails digging deeply into her palms, wished she was a hundred miles away.

"Oh, he's a kind-hearted creature." Loriol's laugh sounded perfectly genuine. "He's rather taken the child under his wing, you know. She's frightfully unsure of herself . . . needs her self-confidence bolstering up a bit. And of course she's terribly naïve. Poor Nicholas even had to tell her when she'd had enough to drink. I've just told him to be careful not to overdo the kind uncle stunt, but he says that she's his good deed for the day!"

What Peta did not know was that Loriol had recognised the evening bag that she had left on the bed and that her sharp eyes had then noticed a slight bulge behind the curtains. Her remarks were meant to be overheard, but to Peta they sounded perfectly spontaneous.

Almost numb with horror, she did not catch Joan

Talbot's reply. Oh, how—how *humiliating*! Loriol's words seemed to echo in her ears, like a record repeating the same phrase over and over again. His good deed for the day. . . ! *That* . . . coming on top of her sudden stupendous discovery that she had fallen hopelessly and shamefully in love for the first time in her life!

The walls of the cottage seemed to be stifling her. She waited until Loriol and Joan Talbot had left the bedroom, then ran swiftly downstairs and out into the garden, unobserved. Perilously near to tears, she was grateful for the cold air on her hot cheeks and prickly eyelids. Someone with a little more conceit of herself might have queried the truth of Loriol's words, but it never occurred to Peta to do so. She was in such a state of confusion and stress and mental conflict that she could hardly think straight, anyway. Discovering that she loved Nicholas had been bad enough, but the other. . . !

"Peta!" She spun round like a startled fawn to find Nicholas, the very last person she wanted to see, standing beside her. His voice was full of concern as he said, "I've been looking for you everywhere. No one seemed to know where you'd gone." Then, catching a glimpse of her white, strained face, "What is it? Don't you feel well?"

He put his hand on her arm as he spoke, but she jerked away, her cheeks flaming. She flung back her head in her old gesture of boyish bravado as she said passionately, "There's no need for you to concern yourself! I can take care of myself!"

There was a moment's silence. Then, "Of course you can," Nicholas said equably. "All the same, you've been missing for nearly an hour. You can't blame me for feeling a little worried about you."

"Overdoing the kind uncle stunt. . . ."

"Oh, mind your own business! Stop treating me like a child, though I know that's how you think of me!" Her voice broke. "A silly, ignorant child!"

Nicholas sucked in his breath and took a step towards her. His expression was suddenly grim.

"Look, what is all this? What did Mike say to you when we were dancing?"

She gave a hysterical little laugh. "Nothing—nothing at all! I've just woken up to a few facts, that's all!"

"Said facts being that I regard you as a child?" Infuriatingly, there was suddenly a tremor of laughter in the deep voice. "My dear, dear Peta, I assure you that it's a very long time since I've thought of you as——"

She did not let him finish. She said passionately, "Oh, go away! Go away . . . *Uncle* Nicholas!"

There was a moment's electrifying silence. The next moment his hands gripped her above the elbows and he said, very deliberately, "I was about to say, Peta, if you'd given me a chance to finish, that it's a long time since I've thought of you as anything but a woman . . . a beautiful, desirable woman. And to prove it. . . ."

Before she realised what he intended to do he had pulled her into his arms. His lips touched hers as lightly as a breath, then they lingered and moved caressingly over hers. For the first time in her life Peta found herself being kissed, gently, tenderly at first and then with a swift graduation of intensity which robbed her of the power to move, even to think. Her body seemed to melt into his as for a timeless time they stood fused together.

At last he raised his head. Drawing a long breath, he looked down into her upturned face and said huskily, "Well, do you know *now* how I feel about you? Do you still believe that I think of you as a child?"

She tried to answer, but couldn't. Her heart was beating with great heavy thumps against her ribs. He was still holding her closely . . . so closely that in the brilliant moonlight she could see a little muscle beating in his hard brown face. There was a long golden hair on the shoulder of his dinner jacket. Loriol's . . . no one else she knew had hair the colour of burnished gold. Realisation flooded her being. With a choked little cry she wrenched herself free. For a moment she stood staring at him, her eyes enormous in her pale face, then she whirled round and ran back towards the house as if pursued by demons. She heard his voice calling her, but she did not stop.

The Harveys, a couple who lived in a cottage near Greylings, were just leaving the party and she ran straight up to them. Making a desperate effort to sound normal, she said, "Please . . . would you mind giving me a lift home? I—I don't want to wait for the others. I—I've got a fearful headache."

If it wasn't true at that precise moment it was certainly true an hour later. Wide-eyed and sleepless, she lay in bed pressing her hands hard against her eyes, trying to will the pain away. Inside her wincing brain still whirled and jostled the thoughts and images which had been torturing her since her return from Cedar Lodge. She loved Nicholas . . . oh, she loved him! She'd loved him for a long time, only she hadn't known it. And . . . he? Despite Loriol, surely he couldn't have kissed her like that, with that deep, aching passion, unless. . . ?

But here her thoughts came to a full stop as a fresh spasm of pain jagged through her head. It was no good, she would have to fetch the aspirins from the bathroom. She wouldn't disturb anyone, Nicholas and Loriol had returned from the party at least an hour ago and the whole house was now silent and sleeping. Sleep . . . that was what she wanted more than anything in the world just at this moment. When she woke up the pain would be gone and she would be able to think more clearly.

She got out of bed and padded noiselessly to the door. As she stepped out on to the landing she stood still, thinking for one crazy moment that she could hear the sound of whispering. She listened, but all was still. She gave herself a mental shake. She must be in a pitiable state, she was even hearing things now!

It wasn't really dark. She made her way along to the bathroom and groped for the aspirins without putting on the light. She was about to return to her own room, the bottle clutched safely in her hand, when suddenly she froze in her tracks. The door on the right of her bedroom . . . Nicholas's bedroom . . . was opening. A moment later a figure stepped out on to the landing and glided swiftly across the corridor to the room opposite. Loriol, in the exquisite, filmy negligée she had worn the night she had visited her, Peta, in her bedroom. Only this time she had been on a different errand. This time she had been with Nicholas.

Peta went to work the next morning with such heavily circled eyes and such a white face that Marjorie, after one startled glance, choked back the breezy question that had been trembling on her lips. How could she possibly ask the child if she had enjoyed the party when she looked as though any moment she might burst into tears?

Insead, she left her severely alone, a kindness for which Peta was enormously grateful. Feeling as angry and ashamed and sick as if it was she herself who had been caught out in some questionable action, she tried desperately to blot out the events of the previous night, but it was impossible. The mental picture of Loriol leaving Nicholas's room seemed indelibly printed on her mind. It seemed that even if Nicholas did not particularly want a wife he was not in the least averse to a little furtive lovemaking. She remembered the tenderness with which he had kissed her, out in the garden of Cedar Lodge, and writhed inwardly, taut with self-disgust. How *could* she have fallen in love with him? She was as bad as Mike . . . just as easily deluded! The only difference was that now she knew the truth she meant to stamp on *her* love. It might take a long time, but she would blot it out, in the end, as completely and finally as if it had never existed.

The morning went by, occupying the surface of her mind but leaving an unhappy turmoil beneath. Stephen Norwell and his brother . . . a pleasant, square-chinned man with a brisk, assured manner . . . were coping with the pupils today and she and Marjorie were occupying themselves with jobs around the boathouse. She was coiling some rope which had been left in a higgledy-piggledy heap when a shadow suddenly fell across her path and she looked up, startled, to find Nicholas standing beside her.

He said quietly, and without any preamble, "I'd like to talk to you, Peta."

Her throat felt tight and dry. She said stiffly, "I'm paid to work, not to talk."

"I'm aware of that. I'll book an hour's instruction with you and we'll find some quiet backwater where we won't be disturbed. I've got some explaining to do: it won't take long, but I want you to listen."

To Peta, stiff with tension, his self-assurance seemed almost arrogant. She missed the glint of anxiety in his grey eyes: she saw only that his jaw was squarer than usual and that, standing over her as he was, he looked frighteningly big and solid.

She said in a choked voice, "There's nothing for us to say to each other. Didn't you get the message last night? I—I don't want anything to do with you. I—I hated you kissing me! It was horrid!"

She wished she hadn't said that. It sounded childish. She wished it more than ever when he answered her.

"Perhaps I'm being unduly conceited, but that isn't the impression you gave me at the time!" There was a quiver of laughter in his voice and when she looked up she thought she saw amusement in his eyes.

Stung, she retorted hotly, not caring what she said as long as she salved her pride and wiped that smile off his face.

"Yes, I shut my eyes and pretended it was Mike!"

It worked. She saw his face, eyes, go suddenly blank. When he next spoke his voice was completely flat and expressionless.

"I—see. Perhaps in that case I needn't apologise for foisting my attentions upon you. It seems I served a purpose, however unflattering I may find it."

He gave her a casual nod and walked away, his back very straight. Peta found herself rooted to the spot, watching his tall figure disappear into the distance and struggling with a feeling which was a combination of sick misery and puzzled frustration. What had brought him here this morning? and what was it that he had wanted to explain to her? The reason for that unexpected kiss in the garden last night? Well, he might have been able to explain *that* away as a mixture of moonlight and midsummer madness, but what about Loriol's presence in his bedroom in the middle of the night? She gave a self-derisive little laugh and returned to her task, concentrating on it so fiercely that when she had finished never had rope been coiled with such scrupulous neatness.

Dinner at Greylings that night might have been an awkward affair, but, owing to the absence of both Nicholas and Loriol, was not. Ann explained that as Loriol had the evening off she had borrowed Nicholas's car and gone off to see a film in Yarmouth, and Nicholas was doing some important revision for the Professor and had asked if he might have his dinner on a tray in the library.

After dinner Peta helped Ann to wash up and then went out into the garden to do some weeding. This was a task she usually avoided, but tonight she felt as though only by dint of sheer hard work would she be able to dull the ache in her heart. (She daren't go to see Richard: he wasn't as blind as Ann.) She was plucking dandelions out of the lawn with something approaching ferocity when, to her dismay, she saw Holly running towards her across the grass.

"Hello, Peta! Doing some hard work for a change?" Holly, wearing blue shorts and shirt, squatted down beside her and felt in her pocket. "Dr. Waring left his cigarette lighter behind last night: at least, we think it's his. It's got his initials on it. Will you give it to him when you see him, please?"

"He's in the library. Why don't you go and give it to him yourself?"

Holly looked at her. "I say, is there anything wrong, Peta? Your voice sounds awfully queer!"

"Does it? Perhaps I'm tired after last night." Peta forced a laugh.

"Did you enjoy yourself? Mum says you left without saying goodnight."

"Yes. I'm sorry. I had a bad headache."

Holly hesitated. Then she said with a rush, "Dickon thinks you were upset because Mike wasn't bowled over by the new you. All the same, if it's any consolation I think the end of the Loriol-Mike affair is within sight. She was simply horrid to him last night, she wouldn't even let him take her home. She went with Dr. Waring instead. You know, Peta, I think I was right and she has been trying to make him jealous! Did you see them dancing together? They made a marvellous combination!"

Peta said nothing, just went on weeding as though it were a matter of life or death.

Holly shuffled uneasily from one foot to the other. She knew something was wrong, and could think of only one reason.

She said desperately, "I'm *sure* Mike will come back to you in the end, Peta! When she's gone everything will be like it used to be!"

Peta's self-control suddenly snapped. "Oh, Holly, stop!" she said, and burst into tears.

If the earth's foundations had given way Holly could not have been more surprised or shocked. In all the years she had known Peta she'd never seen her cry, wouldn't even have believed that she *could*.

"Go away!" Peta sobbed. "Oh, Holly, please leave me alone! Go—go and give Nicholas his lighter!"

A subdued, almost frightened Holly obeyed. Her face was so grave when she accosted Nicholas that he, used to her smiles and dimples, immediately asked what was wrong.

"I'm worried about Peta," Holly said forlornly. She liked and trusted Nicholas and it did not occur to her to prevaricate.

"Worried? Why?" Nicholas asked sharply.

"She's crying, and Peta *never* cries. It's Mike. He's broken her heart," said Holly, her instinct for dramatisation getting the better of her.

Nicholas picked up a paperweight and balanced it between his fingers. "Did she tell you that?"

"Well, as good as. She's loved Mike nearly all her life, you know. They were on the point of getting engaged when Loriol came along." Holly really believed she was telling the truth. "She's ruining Peta's life. It isn't fair, she doesn't really want Mike, but he can't seem to see that she's only playing. I wish to goodness Peta's guardian would hurry up and finish his old book! She'd go away then, and Mike would go back to Peta and everyone would be happy again!"

"An over-simplification, I fear," Nicholas said dryly, but his eyes were thoughtful. For some time after Holly had left him he sat staring out of the window, then, as if acting upon a sudden resolution, he drew a sheet of paper towards him and began to write.

At the end of the next week—a strange week during which Peta took great care to be at home as little as possible—Ann dropped a bombshell. Nicholas, she told Peta, was leaving Greylings on Sunday to stay with relatives before joining the South American archaeological expedition in the autumn. ('What relatives?' thought Peta. 'He told me he hadn't got any!')

Before she had had time to recover from the shock of this announcement Ann followed it up with another.

"And Miss Kent is leaving, too."

"Loriol?"

"Yes. John is very upset, but of course there's nothing he can do about it. She's been offered a job as secretary to a film producer—somebody Dr. Waring knows—with the opportunity for foreign travel and meeting a lot of famous people. Apparently she finds the prospect irresistible, and I can't say I'm surprised. I always thought she'd find it too quiet here, though John seemed to feel that it would work out all right. Luckily Dr. Waring thinks he's found somebody who will be willing to take her place: a far older woman who sounds as though she might be quite satisfactory. She's the widow of an archaeologist, so she won't find the work unfamiliar."

Peta turned away so that Ann should not see her face. Life without Nicholas. . . ? Even now, despite everything, she shrank from the prospect. Instead, she concentrated on thinking about what Loriol's departure would mean to Mike. Almost certainly, the final disillusionment. There wouldn't be room in her glamorous new life for anyone from a tiny Broadlands village. Would there be room for Nicholas? Yes, he'd probably be able to have his cake and eat it too. Still no permanent ties, but always a beautiful woman in the background of his life. This new job was probably something of a compromise. Then, later on, if the compromise didn't work. . . .

She had seen very little of Loriol since Margaret Mandeville's party, but that night the elder girl brought some coffee cups into the kitchen just as she and Ann were about to wash up.

"Well, Peta, heard the news?"

"Yes. I hope you'll be very happy in your new job." Peta spoke steadily, and with an unconscious dignity which gave Ann a jolt. It wasn't just the clothes and hair style which had made Peta seem so grown-up the other night, she thought: she had matured in every way. She went into the dining room to finish clearing away the table and so she missed what followed.

"I'll leave it to you to console poor Mike." Loriol's lively, mocking air said much that was offensive. "Have you ever heard of catching someone on the rebound? It happens, you know."

Peta drew a deep breath. At least Loriol didn't know about her stupid, shameful love for Nicholas! Thank goodness she'd managed to hide *that*! She said coolly, "I'll bear it in mind."

"I wish you would." Loriol flicked an imaginary speck of dirt off her skirt. "Nicholas is quite worried about your future, you know. You haven't been very pleasant to him just lately, but he's really rather fond of you. I think he'd like you to be happy." The red lips curved into a smile. "We'll await with interest the announcement of your wedding!"

"And I yours!" Peta couldn't resist that retort even though she knew that in making it she was hurting herself.

She had the satisfaction of seeing Loriol colour slightly, but just at that moment Ann returned and there was no further opportunity for conversation. That was, in fact, the last time she saw Loriol alone before her departure for London. She carefully contrived never to be alone with Nicholas at all, and even gave up visiting Richard in case their paths should cross. It wasn't easy, for she had a terrible longing for his presence, for the sound of his voice. Yet, even though her spirits seemed weighted by the dull, deadening wretchedness which had been her lot ever since Margaret's party, she was beginning to learn how to bluff the world. Something else involved in growing up, she thought bitterly, and wished passionately that she could have remained the child of a few months before.

She said a brief goodbye to Nicholas and Loriol the night before they left Greylings, but when she returned from work next day Ann handed her a note, in Nicholas's distinctive, upright handwriting. Her heart beating painfully against her ribs, she opened it in the privacy of her room. It was short and cryptic.

"Remember how we once talked about dreams and delusions?" he wrote. "Mine were certainly the latter, but I hope there's a chance that one day you, at least, will have a dream-come-true. Goodbye and God bless. Nicholas."

What he meant Peta did not know, though she puzzled over it for hours. But then there had always been so much she did not know about Nicholas. She had never been able to understand the motives which prompted most of his actions, and least of all she understood his behaviour on the night of the party and subsequently. None of it made any sense, and she supposed it never would.

Greylings seemed very quiet and empty now that the two guests had departed. John Devlin felt their absence keenly, for Nicholas's friendship had meant a great deal to him and he had grown very fond of Loriol. Without quite knowing why Peta felt sorry for him. Perhaps it was because Loriol had let him down so badly, even as Nicholas had let *her* down. At any rate, to Ann's surprised pleasure she went out of her way to be as helpful as she could, even offering to do some of his typing until the replacement, Mrs. Morrison, arrived.

"Of course I'd have to do it with one finger so I wouldn't be able to get through a lot, but if it's any help——?" she suggested tentatively.

Professor Devlin looked at her over the top of his spectacles. Then, satisfied that the offer was genuine, he said, "There are a couple of chapters which I'd be very glad if you could type out for me. They're not mine, Waring wrote them at my request. They cover an aspect of the dig with which I personally was not involved but which will make a useful addition to the book. If you wouldn't mind doing those——?"

Peta nodded, not trusting herself to speak. The task he had given her would, she thought, be half pain, half pleasure, but in the end she enjoyed the work for its own sake. Nicholas wrote as colourfully as he talked, and long before she had finished typing the two chapters, with their vivid descriptions of the rain-forests of the Gran Pajonal and the trek that he had made into the wilderness in search of the lost remnants of a once mighty civilisation, she was completely enthralled. Yet at the same time she experienced a pang of quite irrational fear. He had talked about one or two theories he wanted to follow up . . . did he intend once more to risk his life in the snake-infested swamps and hungry, fever-haunted wilds he described in such fascinating detail? The thought haunted her. He was lost to her now, but she felt that if anything ever happened to him the aching inside her would never stop.

She heard from Holly that Mike had taken Loriol's departure very badly.

"He's just like a bear with a sore head," Holly said. "He feels that she's made such a fool of him, you see."

Peta did see. She said quietly, "I'm sorry."

"*I'm* not!" Holly tossed her head. "He should have had a bit more sense! I haven't got any sympathy with him at all!"

Peta smiled a little ruefully. "You don't exactly choose who you fall in love with, you know. It just happens."

Holly gave her a quick look. She wanted to say that now that Loriol had removed herself with such dramatic suddenness from Mike's life here was Peta's chance, but the memory of a talk she had had with her mother the night before restrained her unruly tongue. Mrs. Mandeville had been quite definite that the friendship between Peta and her elder son was over for good.

"It will take him some time to forget Loriol and in the meantime his pride won't let him take Peta up again," she had said. "Don't try to bring them together again, Holly—it just won't work."

Peta herself knew that things could never again be quite the same between Mike and herself, but she couldn't help hoping that eventually they might be able to recapture something of their old companionship. Then a chance meeting with Margaret Mandeville in Yarmouth, where she had gone with Ann to do some shopping, made her realise that even this was wishful thinking.

"I'm buying some new shirts and pyjamas for Mike. He'll need them in digs, other people's laundering is apt to be so erratic," Margaret said, smilingly.

"Mike . . . in digs?" Peta echoed her words almost disbelievingly. "You mean he's going away?"

"Yes." Margaret answered her smoothly. "His firm have offered to transfer him to the London office and much to my relief he's jumped at the chance." She turned to Ann. "I do think it's so good for young people to escape from the village environment, don't you, Miss Devlin? I was afraid that Mike would be content to stay in a quiet backwater for the rest of his days, but luckily he seems to have woken up at last to the fact that life has more to offer him than just a muddy river and a sailing dinghy.—He's selling *Romany*, by the way," she added casually for Peta's benefit. "He won't have much time for sailing in future."

She did not attempt to hide her satisfaction. She was sorry that Loriol had made Mike so wretched, but she had never expected anything else and the eventual outcome of the affair was better than her wildest dreams. Once he had settled in London she was sure that Mike would never look back. He would fulfil his potential at last.

To Peta, the news that Mike was selling his beloved *Romany,* the dinghy in which they had both spent so many happy hours, meant the severance of the last link with her childhood. She felt tears smarting her eyelids, but her smile when she said goodbye was so gay that Margaret, who had had a few qualms about her, was completely reassured. Holly had told her that Peta was heartbroken about Mike . . . goodness, what nonsense that child talked! It was high time that she learned to keep her inventive imagination within bounds!

CHAPTER ELEVEN

RICHARD MAYNE left for Switzerland at the beginning of September and Mike followed almost immediately afterwards for London. Peta saw him once before he left, but he was with the rest of his family and there was no opportunity for a private talk. Not that she'd wanted one. Mike's hurt was still raw and they had nothing, at the present time, to say to each other.

There followed for Peta the loneliest period of her whole life. Mrs. Morrison, Loriol's replacement, had arrived at Greylings and Professor Devlin, finding to his delight that she was extremely capable, was now forging ahead with his opus. Peta's help was no longer needed, and since it was now the tail-end of the season she was finding that even at the School it was becoming increasingly difficult to keep herself occupied all day.

In late September Marjorie told her, reluctantly, that they were closing down and that her services were no longer required.

"I do wish we could afford to keep you on all through the winter," Marjorie said, looking distressed. "But we've had a hard job as it is to break even, and financially it's impossible."

"That's all right. I knew when I took the job on that it was purely seasonal," Peta assured her.

"What will you do?" Marjorie was still looking anxious, for both she and her husband were fond of Peta and wanted to see her happily settled in a congenial job.

"I'll find something." Peta's smile was confident, but in actual fact she felt completely apathetic about the future. Her guardian was still strongly advocating a secretarial training and though the prospect still did not appeal she sometimes felt that she might do a great deal worse.

Ann had hopefully suggested a domestic science course. "It may come in very useful, you know, dear," she said wistfully.

"Meaning that you plan to abdicate and leave me to look after Greylings?" Peta asked, laughing.

"Well, dear, when you get married. . . ." Ann began, and then stopped, going pink.

Dear old blunderbuss Ann! Peta thought ruefully. The penny had dropped, even with her. She'd stopped lamenting Mike's sudden departure and no longer asked, every time the postman came, if he'd written.

During her last week with the Norwells Peta wrote to Richard Mayne telling him, among other things, that she would soon be out of a job and that her future plans were uncertain. A reply came promptly, but from Celia and not from him.

"If you're really undecided what to do why don't you come and stay with us while you think things over?" Celia wrote. "In point of fact, if it would help you to feel that you were completely independent and standing on your own two feet, you could be of the greatest help to me with the children. I still haven't been able to find a really satisfactory nanny for them, and someone like yourself would be an absolute blessing. *Do* come, Peta! We'd simply love to have you and I think you yourself might quite enjoy being here. We're a reasonably happy family—except when the boys are utterly fiendish, and luckily that isn't *too* often!—and this is a heavenly spot. We can't offer you sailing, I'm afraid, but there'll be plenty of skiing and skating later on, and Father is quite sure that you'd excel at both!"

It was, Peta knew, an invitation that most people would jump at. That evening she went for a long tramp by herself over the lonely marshes and came to a decision. Although her surroundings were as dear and familiar as ever, she had lost practically everything else—the job she had enjoyed doing, the friend whose interests she had shared, and the man whom she had loved. There was nothing and nobody to hold her here now, except perhaps Ann, and even she would not really miss her, with the Professor and Mrs. Morrison safely ensconced for the winter. (Ann liked Mrs. Morrison: she was a kindred spirit. She even shared Ann's passion for gardening.)

167

When Peta went home she announced that after careful consideration she had decided to accept Celia's offer. The Professor was delighted—himself an inveterate globe-trotter, he considered that foreign travel was the best thing out for broadening the mind—and Ann was unselfish enough to feel relieved. The wistful look in Peta's hazel eyes was worrying her. Like everyone else she thought that the girl was pining for Mike, and hoped that a few months in Switzerland would not only bring forgetfulness but also a new beginning.

Peta had no such hopes, but even she felt a stir of excitement as she caught her first glimpse of the spectacular Swiss scenery. Accustomed to a flat landscape, the main features of which were windmills and reeds and slow rivers plaiting reflections, she arrived at Lucerne almost dazed by all that she had seen. Dazzling white mountains standing out against the bluest of skies, dark forests contrasting with bright green meadows down the hillsides and reaching to the shores of wide lakes of ever-changing colour, purple, blue and green—it all added up to something entirely different from anything she had ever known.

Celia and her husband, a pleasant-looking man whose quiet manner contrasted sharply with his wife's bubbling vivacity, were at Lucerne to meet her.

"Oh, Peta, how nice to see you again! I *am* glad you've come!" Celia, slim and very attractive in a light woollen suit and a rakish little hat, greeted her with a warmth which effectively dispelled her slight touch of shyness. "This is Louis, as I expect you've already gathered. Yes, Father is quite all right"—forestalling Peta's anxious question. "He's tons better than he was, and looking forward to seeing you. He would have come with us to meet you, but Louis' car is being serviced and we thought that if you'd got piles of luggage it might be a tight squeeze in my little car."

"Not piles. Just two suitcases," Peta said, laughing. She hadn't been able to afford many new clothes, but just before she had left Norfolk her guardian had surprised her by presenting her with an almost embarrassingly large cheque.

"I want you to enjoy yourself. No need for you to be short of money," he'd said gruffly as she thanked him. Both were aware that a better understanding existed between them, though neither knew quite how it had come about.

It was not far to the Montel's luxury chalet on the shore of the beautiful Lake. It was, as Celia had said in her letter, a 'heavenly spot', though Louis pointed out with a smile that Peta had really come at the wrong time of year.

"Oh, but Switzerland is beautiful at any time," Celia protested. She looked at Peta. "Father is having the time of his life, as you can probably imagine. He's doing some really good work. Lovely portraits of the boys—though heaven knows how he managed to get them to sit still for more than five seconds!—and some gorgeous landscapes. I've told him that he'll have enough to hold an exhibition soon!"

Richard was, indeed, at his easel when they arrived. Peta realised at once that Celia had not exaggerated and that he did look a lot healthier. There was more spring in his step and his eyes were clear and bright.

"You see before you a happy man," he said, smiling, when Peta exclaimed at his changed appearance. "And you, my dear? Let me have a look at you." He put his hands on her slender shoulders and turned her round to face the light, his gaze suddenly intent. Peta met his eyes bravely, though she coloured a little under his scrutiny.

"H'm." If Richard was dissatisfied with what he saw he did not show it. Instead he said lightly, "I see you've become a young lady of fashion. Very nice, too—but what's happened to the old blue denims? Not consigned to the dust-heap, I hope?"

Peta managed to smile. So much of her life had been consigned to the dust-heap, but not the blue denims.

Over tea, a friendly, comfortable meal, Peta met the two little boys, Matthew and Jean, and their unofficial 'nursemaid', Karen, who was a rosy-faced girl with kind eyes. Despite their mother's assertions regarding their characters, Peta found the children delightful and they were soon swarming all over her, quick to realise that they had found a new friend.

Eventually Celia rescued her in order to show her over the house, which fulfilled the promise of its attractive exterior. All the rooms, though luxuriously appointed and furnished, had a 'home-like' atmosphere and all the big picture windows looked out on to splendid views. The charming bedroom allotted to Peta was at the front of the house and looked out on to towering, snow-capped mountains.

She thought of the view from her own window at home. Its place in her heart was secure, but of course it couldn't be compared with this glorious scenery. For some time she stood with her nose pressed against the glass, her eyes fixed on the white peaks which sparkled in the late afternoon sunshine as if they were frosted with diamonds. They looked remote and unattainable. Perhaps that was why Nicholas loved mountains so—they presented a challenge, the challenge of the unknown.

She realised, with a little shock of surprise, that for an hour or two she had actually managed to forget Nicholas, and the suddenness of remembering again was almost a physical pain. If only he was with her here now . . . But no, he was already on his way to Peru. The Professor had received a card from him just before he left. No doubt Loriol had been at the airport to say goodbye to him, she thought bitterly.

She gave herself a mental shake and started to do her unpacking. At the bottom of one suitcase she found the gift that she had received from Richard before he left for Switzerland. It was one of his pictures, and the one she had liked best, of the wild geese flying over the marshes. She proceeded to hang it beside her bed, feeling that even in Switzerland she was entitled to a little bit of her beloved Norfolk. Who knew how long it would be before she saw it again?

Peta quickly settled down to her new life with the Montels and by the time a few weeks had passed she felt very much one of the family. She and Celia had become firm friends, she liked Louis and she loved the children, and she was glad to find that the sympathy which had always existed between her and Richard was as real as it had ever been.

Her surroundings—the towering mountains, wide-spread forests, green slopes, orchards and meadows and beautiful Lake, with its soft blue distances and deep shadows—appealed strongly and she spent much of her time walking and climbing, either by herself or with Celia and the children. There was, however, another side to the coin. Louis' position required him to do a great deal of entertaining, and Peta soon found that she was expected to take part in what she rather ruefully described to Ann, in one of her letters home, as a 'whirl of gaiety'. Luckily her French improved to the point where she no longer found conversation impossible and gradually, under Celia's gentle and unobstrusive influence, she lost her shyness and gaucherie and learned some self-possession.

Looking at her, Richard often reflected how quickly his prophecy had come true. Wearing plain, tailored clothes that Celia helped her to choose, her hair cut and set in an attractive new style (she'd grow it again if Ann didn't like it, she said) and her make-up carefully applied to enhance her golden-brown tan and vivid colouring, she seemed a very different girl from the long-legged, brown ragamuffin he had first known. Different outwardly, at least. Much to his delight her personality was unchanged. She had all her old warmth and vitality, though sometimes, when she thought she was unobserved, he noticed a wistful curve to her lips and a faraway look in her eyes. So she hadn't forgotten her young Viking even now, he thought grimly.

Peta herself was dismayed to find that despite all her valiant efforts to efface Nicholas from her memory he was never far away from her thoughts. Not but that there weren't several very attractive and eligible young men only too willing to lay his ghost. She never lacked invitations, but rarely accepted them. None of her would-be escorts really attracted her, though there was one possible exception. His name was Stefan Seiler

171

and he was a fair-haired, blue-eyed young giant whose parents were friends of Richard's. A junior partner in his father's flourishing textile firm, he spoke fluent English and excelled at nearly all sports.

Peta liked him because he reminded her in so many ways of Mike, and for a time they enjoyed what she, at least, believed to be a cheerful, uncomplicated friendship. Matthew and Jean often accompanied them on their outings, and when the first snow came it was Stefan who taught them all to ski and Stefan who guided their first faltering steps on the ice. Peta, in particular, was an apt pupil, and it was not long before she was able to leave the nursery slopes and skim wherever she pleased in an undulating, white world bathed in sunlight.

She had intended to return to Greylings for Christmas, but Celia had a bad bout of 'flu in mid-December which left her so weak and listless that Peta decided to change her plans. Stefan and his parents came over to spend Boxing Day with the Montels, and it was then that Stefan, his fluent English for once deserting him, asked Peta to marry him.

For perhaps one moment she was tempted to say yes. Stefan was so nice and so kind, and she liked him so much. If she married him there would be no more uncertainty about the future . . . no more wondering what she should do with her life when she returned to England. Then, fiercely, she upbraided herself. Stefan deserved to be more than somebody's second-best, and it was useless to deny what her heart told her. No matter how hard she'd tried to forget Nicholas, how much she'd forced herself to stop loving him, she hadn't yet succeeded. She couldn't marry anyone else under those circumstances.

Inevitably the Montels heard of Peta's decision from Stefan's parents. They were all disappointed, and several days later Richard, after considerable hesitation, brought the matter up.

Carefully packing his pipe, he said quietly, "Peta, my dear, be as sharp as you please with me if you think I'm an interfering old busybody. You can consign me to the devil if you like. But are you still carrying the torch for Mike Mandeville? Is that why you've refused to marry Stefan?"

Peta looked at him in almost shocked surprise. She and Richard had become so close that somehow it had never occurred to her that he was labouring under such a misconception.

"Carrying the torch for Mike?" she repeated. Then, a little incoherently, "Oh, Richard, no! I—I never have!"

Richard raised his brows. "You never have? But, my dear——"

Peta, her face scarlet, interrupted him. "Mike was never anything more to me than a very dear friend. I liked him enormously—better than anyone else. But I was never in love with him—*never!*"

There was no mistaking her passionate sincerity. After one startled moment Richard said slowly, "My dear, I'm sorry. I quite thought . . . I was sure . . ." He stopped helplessly.

Peta said unsteadily, "It's a mistake a lot of people made. I suppose it was natural. We'd always been together so much."

"Then you haven't refused to marry Stefan because there's someone else?"

Peta's eyes filled with tears. Distractedly she said, "Stefan is a dear, but I just don't love him. I—I wish I did."

She hadn't answered his question, Richard thought. He was too courteous and too kind-hearted to pursue the matter in the face of her obvious distress, but it niggled at the back of his mind. She might not have been in love with Mike Mandeville, but there'd been someone, he was quite sure of that. If it wasn't Mike, then who had it been?

The answer to his puzzled question came quite unexpectedly a few days later. Peta was helping Louis to take down the Christmas decorations when Celia, who was immersed in a copy of the Continental *Daily Mail*, gave a sudden exclamation.

"Gracious! This should interest you, Peta! Loriol

Kent, the girl who worked for your uncle and who was at school with me, has just got married. Look, here's her photograph. I must say I wouldn't have recognised her: she's certainly a raving beauty!"

Peta, who was standing on a chair, her hands full of silver and golden filigree balls, swayed and went so deathly white that Richard thought she was going to faint. He sprang to his feet, but Louis, who was nearest, had already rushed to her side. He caught hold of her and lifted her down, keeping a protective arm round her waist.

"Peta! What is the matter? What is wrong?"

Peta brushed an unsteady hand across her eyes. Fighting desperately for self-control, she said unsteadily, "I'm sorry. Just a bit dizzy, that's all. I must have been up there a bit too long."

She sank down into a chair next to Celia and tried to smile.

"What was that you were saying? Loriol's married? I—I'm not surprised. I knew that she and Nicholas were on the point of being engaged when they were at Greylings."

Celia stared at her. "Nicholas? Who's he? Who said anything about Nicholas?"

Peta gave a cracked little laugh. "Well, since he's the bridegroom. . . ."

"But he isn't." Celia, looking completely bewildered, handed the paper over. "She's married Zack Montague, the Hollywood film producer. Four times married already and a millionaire several times over, hence all the ballyhoo, I presume. He's quite a catch by certain standards!"

Dazed and disbelieving, Peta looked down at the newspaper. That was unmistakably Loriol's beautiful face smiling up at her, but the man at her side . . . stout, heavy-jowled, balding and fifty if he was a day . . . no, that certainly wasn't Nicholas!

Richard, watching the colour creep slowly back into her pale cheeks, gave a soundless little whistle. *Waring!* Of course! He could have kicked himself for not having had the sense to realise it before. Except . . . except

174

that whoever it was that Peta loved had so obviously caused her pain and disillusionment, and Waring hadn't struck him as that sort of man. He hadn't seen much of him, it was true, but what little he had seen he had liked tremendously.

He frowned to himself. No, he couldn't believe that his instincts had been that wrong. Waring wouldn't have consciously hurt the child. But——poor little Peta! No doubt about it, she was still crazy about the bloke. Even though he was thousands of miles away, she hadn't forgotten him.

Peta, mercifully unaware how completely she had given herself away, was thinking hard. Loriol must have grown tired of waiting for Nicholas to make up his mind and Zack Montague and his millions had proved too much of a temptation. Well, she was glad. Nicholas, whatever his morals, deserved a far better wife than Loriol would ever have been. She wondered if he knew. Probably not, if he was in the wilds of Peru. Perhaps, though, he wouldn't even mind very much. A man as attractive as Nicholas Waring could always find a replacement, she reminded herself bitterly.

In the months that followed Peta thought long and hard about her future. Celia begged her to stay on in Switzerland, insisting that her help with home and family was invaluable, but this as a permanent arrangement did not suit Peta's independent spirit. Eventually she decided to return to England some time in March and to start investigating the possibility of a horticultural training. She wasn't a fanatical gardener, like Ann, but at least it was a job which would keep her out of doors. (She had decided to put all thoughts of returning to her old job out of her mind. Marjorie, writing jubilantly to announce the safe arrival of Annabel——only it wasn't Annabel, it was Christopher!——had mentioned that Stephen's brother was going into partnership with them, so her help wouldn't really be needed.)

Richard, too, was making plans. He had decided to make his home permanently in Switzerland, but was busy arranging an exhibition of his paintings which was to be held in London in mid-March. Several portraits were being hung, including Peta's, and all his Swiss and Norfolk landscapes.

"You won't sell Peta's portrait, will you?" Celia asked, and looked relieved when Richard shook his head.

"I ought to mark it N.F.S., but I think I shall put a price on it, just for fun. Although it's one of the best things I've ever done no one will want to pay as much as I shall ask, and so it will be quite safe. I think, though, that it may amuse little Peta, when she visits the exhibition, to see how highly I value her portrait. She was very much afraid that in painting her I was wasting my time!"

The exhibition was due to be opened on the fourteenth of March, and Richard, with strict instructions from Celia not to over-tire himself, left Switzerland a week before to arrange the necessary details. Since Louis had a week's leave owing to him he and Celia decided to spend it in London, so that they could travel with Peta and not only visit the exhibition but also show Matthew and Jean all the sights.

"They've never been to England before. It's high time they saw the Tower and Buckingham Palace and the Zoo and—oh, all the other places that tourists flock to!" Celia told Peta. "I wish we could persuade you to join our sight-seeing tour! I'm sure you don't know half as much about London as you ought to!"

Peta shook her head, smiling. "I must go home. I've been away more than five months, remember."

"Is your guardian still at Greylings?"

"Yes, but he'll be off again soon, Ann says. The book is practically finished, only about one more chapter to do."

(Ann wrote frequently, but though in one of her letters she had mentioned that she had seen an account of Loriol's wedding, she never referred to Nicholas. Or Mike, though Holly had written to say that the family was moving to Hayes, in Kent, in order to be nearer London. Apparently the uncle to whom Cedar Lodge had belonged had died suddenly, leaving the property to Margaret Mandeville, so that there were no longer any financial barriers.)

"Well, you must visit Father's exhibition before you go home," Celia said firmly. "He'd never forgive you if you didn't."

"I wouldn't dream of missing it. Perhaps I'll stay one night in London with you and Louis and travel down to Norfolk the next day."

"A good idea," Celia agreed, and thus it was arranged.

When the time came Peta felt a pang of genuine regret in saying goodbye to Switzerland, which she had come to love. That feeling of regret was intensified when, after a short but bumpy flight, they arrived in London on what was a particularly bleak and cheerless winter's day. To Peta, the city seemed inordinately grey and drab and dirty after the immaculate cleanliness of the Swiss towns, and she couldn't help wishing that she could go straight home. Except, of course, that if she did so Richard would be disappointed, and she wouldn't hurt him for worlds.

As it turned out she visited the exhibition alone, for Celia wanted to go with Louis and because of a business engagement he was unable to make an immediate visit. Not without a certain amount of difficulty Peta found her way to the little gallery which for one week was being given over entirely to Richard's collection, and was glad to see that there were people coming and going all the time. Richard often described himself as a 'has-been', but that wasn't true. His work was still very much admired and respected.

Mingling with the crowds, she heard their comments on the various pictures with amused interest and stored some of them up to recount to Richard later. The Swiss landscapes seemed to be the most popular, but after five months of mountains and their crystalline brilliance she found the Norfolk landscapes, with their muted colours, singularly restful. She stood in front of the latter, staving off a wave of homesickness by reminding herself how soon she would be back at Greylings, when a familiar voice spoke at her shoulder.

"Peta! It *is* Peta, isn't it?" Then, as she turned round, her eyes wide with surprise, "Yes, it is! I wasn't quite sure at first."

"Mike!" He was the last person she had expected to see and she was completely lost for words.

He grinned at her, and it was his old friendly grin, though otherwise she thought he had changed a lot. He had lost his healthy tan and many of his freckles with it, and he was conventionally dressed in a dark suit and sober tie. And—yes, he was carrying a briefcase.

"I've been staring at you for ages. Instinct told me it was you, though I found it hard to believe." His gaze dwelt significantly on her fashionable navy blue coat with its white woollen collar and white buttons and belt and the navy and white silk scarf tied in a new gipsy style round her short copper hair.

Peta coloured. "What are you doing here? I didn't think pictures were much in your line. At least, they weren't in the old days." ("Old days"? Five months ago? Well, it felt like aeons, she thought.)

"They're not, but someone told me that these Norfolk landscapes were rather good, so I decided to come and have a look-see. I miss the old place, you know: Mother and the kids moved to Hayes a couple of weeks ago, so I don't even go back for an occasional weekend now." He drew a deep breath which sounded suspiciously like a sigh, then added, "Anyway, what about you? Mother said you were in Switzerland."

"I came back today. I'm going home tomorrow."

Mike laughed. "I suppose you wanted to admire your portrait? It's over there: the first thing I saw when I walked in. It's jolly good: people have been raving about it. I might even have felt like buying it, for old times' sake, if I'd been in the millionaire class!"

He led her over to the portrait as he spoke, then showed her the price marked against the picture in the catalogue. Her eyes widened incredulously.

"But he can't possibly expect to sell it at that price!"

"It's sold." A woman standing next to them heard

Peta's startled comment and turned round to put her right. "Not half an hour ago. I know, because I was buying a small landscape at the same time. It was a man who bought it, he wrote out a cheque there and then without turning a hair." Her eyes widened suddenly as she noticed the resemblance between Peta and the portrait. "I say! Aren't you the girl—" but Peta, scarlet, had already fled, Mike at her heels.

"Clever of her, wasn't it?" said Mike, trying unsuccessfully to hide his amusement at Peta's embarrassment. "Though, come to think of it, you haven't changed all that much. It's the clothes that make all the difference, I suppose."

He glanced at his watch. "Look here, have you seen enough? Would you like a quick cup of coffee? It's all I've got time for, I'm afraid, but there's something I'd like to tell you."

Peta gave him a quick look. "No inquest, Mike?"

He shook his head and took hold of her arm as they walked along the pavement. "No inquest, Peta. But I'd like to tell you how sorry I am for the way I behaved last summer. I treated you abominably, though I didn't realise it at the time." His lips twisted a little. "There was quite a lot I didn't realise, I'm afraid."

"It wasn't altogether your fault.—This will do, won't it?" and Peta indicated a small, attractive-looking milk bar.

Mike did not answer until they were seated at a small table with steaming cups of coffee before them. Then he said soberly, "I'm afraid it *was* my fault. I deserved all I got, except—I did love her, you know, Peta. I thought she was the most marvellous girl I'd ever seen in my life. You—and even young Holly— guessed that she was just amusing herself, but I—" He broke off, the shadow of pain on his face. With a stab of compassion Peta thought, "It's as bad for him as it is for me. He hasn't forgotten Loriol any more than I've forgotten Nicholas."

She said quickly, "I only knew because she actually told me that she and Nicholas were in love. She didn't make any secret of it to me, but I had to promise her that I wouldn't say anything to anyone else." She broke off, aware that Mike was staring at her. "What's the matter?"

He said slowly, "Loriol told you that she and Waring were in love? But that simply wasn't true. At least, she might have been keen on him, but he certainly didn't care tuppence about her!"

Peta's lips were suddenly dry. "What do you mean? How do you know?"

Mike looked a little surprised at her intensity, but he answered readily. "Well, you remember the night of the party, when Loriol and Waring went off together and left us high and dry? At the end of that dance Loriol wanted a repeat performance, but I was standing just behind them and I heard Waring tell her that he couldn't, he wanted to find you. Then Loriol said something I didn't catch, but it seemed to get under Waring's skin. He snapped out something pretty brutal about not loving her and never giving her the slightest reason to think he did." He stopped, looking a little uncomfortable. "I suppose I shouldn't have been listening, but I was so beside myself that night that I hardly knew what I was doing. I'd more or less tumbled to the fact that Loriol didn't want to be with me, she wanted to be with Waring, and it was some consolation to know that *he* didn't want *her*!"

"But—" Peta began, and then stopped. She couldn't possibly tell Mike that she had seen Loriol coming out of Nicholas's bedroom. In any case . . . was it possible that she had jumped to the wrong conclusion? She put her hand to her head, almost ashamed of the turmoil which his words had aroused in her. Oh *no,* she thought in horror. It couldn't start again, all that confusion and stress and mental conflict!

Mike did not seem to have noticed her disquiet. He was looking again at his watch: he had, he explained, promised to meet a friend and they were going to a revue together.

"Come and look us up some time, won't you?" he asked. "You know Mum and the kids will be glad to see you. Me too, if I'm at home."

They smiled at each other. Both realised, regretfully, that their old companionship had gone for good and that there was nothing they could put in its place. Both were wise enough not to think, wistfully, of the might-have-been.

For a long time after Mike had left her Peta sat very still, staring into the distance, but eventually she roused herself. Out of sheer curiosity she'd go back to the Gallery and find out whether that woman had been right and whether in fact her portrait *had* been sold for that astronomical figure. She couldn't believe it was possible: someone must have made a mistake!

The first person she saw when she re-entered the Gallery was Richard. He was looking, she thought, extraordinarily excited, quite unlike his usual calm imperturbable self.

Directly he saw her he came hurrying towards her. "Peta, my dear! Your portrait's been sold!"

"I heard it had been: I was here earlier." Peta hesitated. Was that the cause of Richard's excitement? No, she decided. Money—even *that* sort of money—meant nothing to him. Shyly she said, "You didn't want it to be, did you? Celia told me earlier that you didn't want to part with it."

"No, I didn't want to part with it. At least—" Richard stopped. For a moment or two he was silent, as if thinking hard, then he said slowly, "Peta, my dear, would you be prepared to do me a big favour?"

"Of course." Peta looked bewildered. "What is it?"

"Will you take a letter from me to the man who has bought your portrait, asking him if he'll take back his cheque? Oh, I know it isn't done!"—impatiently, as Peta gasped. "But I know the man—slightly—and I think that if I explain the circumstances he'll be prepared to do what I ask."

"All right." Peta spoke reluctantly, for the thought of such an errand filled her with dismay. What on earth was Richard thinking of? Surely the purchaser, whoever he was, would have a right to be furious at such an extraordinary request!—but she could not refuse. She watched, biting her lip, as Richard rapidly scribbled a few lines on a piece of paper and put it into an envelope with the offending cheque.

"That'll teach me a lesson," he said wryly, handing her the envelope after he'd written the address. "I ought to have marked the portrait N.F.S., but I thought it would amuse you to know what value I put upon it."

Peta glanced at the envelope. 23, Albemarle Street.

"It's quite near here. Take a taxi: I'll call one for you," Richard said with unusual briskness, and was gone before Peta could remind him that he hadn't told her the name of the person she had to ask for.

With a shrug she decided not to bother. Whoever lived at 23, Albemarle Street would know who it was who went round paying small fortunes for pictures! Really, she thought indignantly, Richard was behaving most oddly over all this! However much he'd wanted to keep the portrait, a contract was a contract and he had no right to try and break it!

Her destination proved to be a block of flats and No. 23 was about halfway up. She knocked shyly at the door, wondering miserably how on earth she was going to explain her impossible errand, and drew a deep breath as a thin, bespectacled man with tousled hair and a vague expression opened it.

"Excuse me! I wondered—that is, did you by any chance buy a picture at Richard Mayne's exhibition this afternoon?" She did her best to sound self-possessed, but could not help colouring hotly under his surprised and interested gaze.

"Not me, I'm afraid. I've not been out. Don't know about my friend, though. Does some queer things from time to time," he said cheerfully. "Come in and ask him."

He ushered her through a small hall and then into a large, comfortable room with walls packed with shelves of books and brightly coloured rugs on the gleaming oak floor. There was a desk in front of the window, littered with books and papers, and a dark-haired man was sitting at it, his back towards the door.

"Visitor for you, Waring," said the bespectacled one

amiably. "At least, she's not for me, unfortunately, so unless she's got the wrong address you seem to be the lucky one."

He disappeared through the open doorway just as the man at the desk looked round. Peta, after one incredulous, horrified moment of stunned recognition, turned to flee too, but Nicholas was too quick for her. Crossing the room in three hasty strides, he slammed the door shut and stood with his back towards it.

"Peta!" he said slowly, and something in his voice and his eyes made her knees feel as though they were turning into water.

She took refuge in the inane. "I thought—I thought you were in Peru!"

"And I thought you were in Switzerland! At least, that's what the Professsor told me in his last letter! What are you doing here? Why have you come?"

Trying to keep her hand from shaking, Peta held out Richard's letter. "Richard sent me. I didn't know this was for you."

She watched him tear open the envelope and an awful realisation dawned. "Nicholas! It wasn't you . . . who paid all that money . . . for my portrait?" Never before had she found it so difficult to articulate.

He looked up from the note and smiled at her stricken face, his grey eyes glinting.

"Oh, but it was. A very good bargain I made, too. I'm surprised at Mr. Mayne thinking that I might want to go back on it."

Peta's handbag slid out of her hands and fell on to the floor with a little thud.

"Unless," Nicholas added deliberately, "I get something even better in its place. Like—for instance—the real thing."

He took two steps towards her. The next thing she knew his arms were holding her fast and he was kissing her hard. Peta, taken completely by surprise, could hardly bear the violence of that kiss and the emotions it roused in her. Then, suddenly, joy was running through her veins like quicksilver and she was responding to the pressure of his mouth on hers. She forgot the pain and misery of the last few months, asked no inner question now about him or herself. She was in his arms and that was all that mattered.

It was quite some time later that Nicholas stopped kissing her. He held her a little away from him and said huskily, "I love you. D'you hear me, Peta? I love you. I tried to tell you a long time ago, but you wouldn't listen. And now for heaven's sake tell me that what Mayne says is true and that you feel the same way."

"I . . . do." Peta, looking and sounding completely dazed, let the reference to Richard pass.

Nicholas drew a deep breath. "And you let me go away thinking that you loved —Mike Mandeville? Why, darling? Why did you?"

She looked up at him, her eyes wide and dark in her pale face. Her heart was still thundering against her ribs and her voice was unsteady as she said, "Because of Loriol."

She saw his brows shoot up. "Loriol?"

"She told me that you and she—that you were in love, only you didn't want any permanent ties. I—I believed her. It seemed so obvious."

Nicholas said tautly, "She told you that we were in love? And you believed her? Even after that damned party, when I was so much in love with *you* that it was sheer hell being with you and not being able to tell you? I never meant to kiss you that night. I never meant to touch you. I was so sure you were eating your heart out for Mike, you see. But when you called me . . . *Uncle* Nicholas . . . well, I'm human and it was more than I could stand. Afterwards, of course, I thought I'd spoiled everything."

He paused, his voice changing as he felt her give a little shiver. "Darling, you're trembling!" He drew her over to a chair and pulled her on to his knees, his touch as gentle as it had been ruthless before.

"Young Holly didn't help. She told me that Mike had broken your heart and that your only hope was that he'd go back to you after Loriol had gone." His arms tightened round her as she gave a startled protest.

184

"It seemed to make sense. All I had to think of was a bait tempting enough to make her throw in her hand."

He gave a grim little laugh. "I knew, you see, that she wanted to marry me, but I always refused to take her seriously. In fact, her machinations used to amuse me until she started making a play for Mike and I realised that there was a chance that you were going to get hurt. After that, I could cheerfully have wrung her neck!"

"You never showed the way you really felt about her," Peta said reproachfully.

"Little fire-eater! I tried to be nice to her because of her father. He once did me a very good turn and I promised him, in return, that I'd help Loriol if I could. That's why I asked the Professor to take her on as his secretary, though I can't tell you how much I regretted it afterwards. *You* were the only reason I stayed on at Greylings."

He paused. "In a way, perhaps what happened wasn't altogether Loriol's fault. Men had been falling for her charms ever since she was sixteen and she just couldn't bring herself to believe that I simply wasn't interested. Finally, the night of the party, I had to tell her straight out that she was wasting her time." He gave a rueful laugh. "She was so furious that she tore a strip off me all the way home, and even then, when I'd got to bed, she came barging into my room to deliver a final broadside!"

He stopped. "What's the matter? What have I said?"

Peta's eyes had filled with tears and she buried her face against his shoulder. "Oh, Nicholas, I saw her! Coming out of your room! I—I thought——" She stopped, shamefaced, unable to go on.

"You thought the worst!" Nicholas finished the sentence for her. "Well, I'll be damned! I've always suspected that women made themselves an awful lot of trouble by jumping to the wrong conclusions on the most insubstantial evidence, and now I know it! My dear sweet idiot, didn't it ever occur to you that I simply wasn't that sort of man? You seem to have a very low opinion of my morals!"

His voice and eyes were teasing. Peta swallowed to dispel the slight huskiness from her voice and said defensively, "Well, she *is* very beautiful. I always felt such a scruff beside her!"

He smiled at her with great tenderness. "My darling, practically from the first moment I saw you no other woman existed for me. Not that I thought I had a chance—I was sure you were in love with your young Viking."

Peta shook her head. "I never thought of Mike in that way. At least, not until I started feeling miserable and then I wondered. It wasn't for a long time that I realised I was aching for you!"

He gave a laugh that was half a groan. "And we've had half a world between us for the last five months! Oh, Peta!"

He felt her grow suddenly tense. "Nicholas! Why *are* you here? Why aren't you still in Peru? You haven't been ill again, have you?"

His mouth curved. "Silly one! No, it wasn't me this time. I had to fly back, two days ago, with a member of the party who suddenly went down with a mysterious virus infection. David, whom you've just met and who has so tactfully disappeared, is his brother. He offered to put me up until I have to return to Peru."

"When?"

"Probably some time next week." He felt her cling to him and stroked her hair tenderly. "You don't think I'd leave you behind, now that I've found you again, do you? I want you to come with me, darling—as my wife. Does a honeymoon under a mosquito net appeal to you?"

Since he chose that moment to kiss her again, her reply was inaudible. Later, however, he asked anxiously, "Will you mind not having a grand wedding? There won't be time for much of a show, I'm afraid, just a quiet ceremony in your little village church with a few special friends."

"Perfect!" Peta said with satisfaction.

"And after the ceremony you can put off your bridal clothes and wear your old blue denims again, just to please me," Nicholas said, smiling. "We'll hire us a boat and go wherever we fancy, wherever the wind blows free."

Peta suddenly remembered why she had come here in the first place. "Nicholas! What did Richard say in his note? I never told him that I loved you, but he must have planned all this after he'd discovered that you'd practically bankrupted yourself to buy my portrait!"

Nicholas grinned. "He said he couldn't understand what I wanted with a painting when I'd find the real thing so much more satisfactory! Also that if I managed to persuade you to marry me I could have the portrait—as a wedding present!"

His face became suddenly grave as he came up to the last hurdle. "Peta, you know that I'm a nomadic sort of person? My work takes me all over the world, and I won't want to leave you behind. You won't break your heart if our visits to your beloved Broads are few and far between?"

She shook her head. "People matter more than places. I'll be happy wherever you are, Nicholas."

As his arms enfolded her she knew that it was true. Wherever Nicholas's work took him, to whatever far-flung places, one thing would remain constant. Though every day might show them how buildings crumbled, civilisations decayed and ancient glories passed away, they would know that love, true love, was for ever.

A Publishing Event of special interest.

The autobiography of
a warm and charming
woman who has
become one of the
most famous authors
of romantic fiction
in the world

The Essie Summers Story

SEE OVERLEAF FOR DETAILS AND ORDER COUPON

The Essie Summers Story

One of the world's most popular and admired authors of romantic fiction, and a special favourite of all Harlequins readers, tells her story.

Essie Summers, the author of such best selling books as "Bride in Flight", "Postscript to Yesterday", "Meet on my Ground" and "The Master of Tawhai" to name just a few, has spent two years bringing the manuscript of her autobiography to its present stage of perfection.

The wit, warmth and wisdom of this fine lady shine, through every page. Her love of family and friends, of New Zealand and Britain, and of life itself is an inspiration throughout the book. Essie Summers captures the essence of a life well lived, and lived to the fullest, in the style of narrative for which she is justly famous.

"The Essie Summers Story", published in paperback, is available at .95 a copy through Harlequin Reader Service, now!

Have You Missed Any of These

Harlequin Romances?

AA-2